Anonymous

Sixth Annual Report of The County and City of Worcester

Anatiposi

Anonymous

Sixth Annual Report of The County and City of Worcester

Reprint of the original.

1st Edition 2023 | ISBN: 978-3-38230-460-7

Anatiposi Verlag is an imprint of Outlook Verlagsgesellschaft mbH.

Verlag (Publisher): Outlook Verlag GmbH, Zeilweg 44, 60439 Frankfurt, Deutschland
Vertretungsberechtigt (Authorized to represent): E. Roepke, Zeilweg 44, 60439 Frankfurt, Deutschland
Druck (Print): Books on Demand GmbH, In de Tarpen 42, 22848 Norderstedt, Deutschland

SIXTH

ANNUAL REPORT

OF

𝕿𝖍𝖊 𝕮𝖔𝖚𝖓𝖙𝖞 𝖆𝖓𝖉 𝕮𝖎𝖙𝖞

OF

WORCESTER

PAUPER LUNATIC ASYLUM.

WORCESTER:
PRINTED BY CHALK AND HOLL, HERALD-OFFICE, HIGH-STREET.

1859.

Committee of Visitors for 1859.

THE RIGHT HON. LORD WARD, Witley Court, Worcester.

THOS. GALE CURTLER, ESQ., (Chairman), Bevere House, Worcester.

REV. JOHN PEARSON, Suckley, Worcester.

CAPTAIN CANDLER, The Link, Great Malvern.

FRANCIS HOLLAND, ESQ., Cropthorne, Pershore.

COLONEL WOODWARD, The Hyde, Upton-upon-Severn.

J. H. H. FOLEY, ESQ., M.P., Prestwood, Stourbridge.

REV. GEO. R. GRAY, Inkberrow, Alcester.

RICHARD PADMORE, ESQ., Worcester.

THOMAS ROWLEY HILL, ESQ. (Mayor), Worcester.

EDWARD CORLES, ESQ., Worcester.

WM. LEWIS, ESQ., Worcester.

WM. ACTON, ESQ., Wolverton, Worcester.

JOHN SLANEY PAKINGTON, ESQ., Kent's Green, Worcester.

CHAS. R. COXWELL, ESQ., Great Malvern.

Medical Superintendent.

JAMES SHERLOCK, M.D.

Chaplain.

REV. EDWARD HORTON.

Clerk to the Committee of Visitors.

MR. MARTIN CURTLER.

Treasurer.

JOHN WHITMORE ISAAC, ESQ.

Clerk and House Steward.

MR. J. C. HUME.

Matron.

MISS GIDDINGS.

THE SIXTH ANNUAL REPORT

OF THE

COMMITTEE OF VISITORS,

OF THE

COUNTY AND CITY OF WORCESTER PAUPER LUNATIC ASYLUM,

PRESENTED TO THE JUSTICES OF THE COUNTY AT EPIPHANY SESSIONS, 1859, AND TO THE TOWN COUNCIL OF THE CITY, WITHIN TWENTY DAYS OF THE 20TH DAY OF DECEMBER, 1858, PURSUANT TO THE 62ND SECTION OF "THE LUNATIC ASYLUMS ACT, 1853."

YOUR COMMITTEE continue to feel the same confidence in Dr. Sherlock as they have always had, as well as their admiration of the ability, attention, and zeal which he displays in the management of the business of the Asylum, and in the care and treatment of the Patients.

The general conduct of the other officers of the Institution has been satisfactory during the past year.

At our first meeting in the present year, we increased the salary of the Matron from £50 to £60 a-year, and the salary of Mr. Hume, the Asylum Clerk and House Steward, from £100 to £110 per annum. The Matron had served three years, and when engaged was led to expect that at the end of three years an increase of her salary would be made, if her conduct proved satisfactory, which has been so entirely. Mr. Hume has held his office from the opening of the Asylum, and your Committee unanimously considered that his application for an increase of salary was well founded.

As a means of an additional supply of water to the Asylum, we resolved to drain the garden with pipes conducting the water by a main drain into the tanks. The result was, that after 48 hours' rain the tanks were entirely filled. The supply from the roofs of the building had always failed to have that effect. Since the drains have been made, much rain water has in wet weather flowed away in addition to filling the tanks, so that in ordinary seasons an ample supply may·be calculated upon. The unusual absence of rain this year has for some weeks past necessitated the hauling of water from the brook, and therefore it becomes necessary to consider whether additional means for storing the supply of rain water should not be resorted to.

It will be remembered that last year the weekly pay for the Patients was reduced from 10s. 6d. to 9s. 6d. We have now the pleasure to state that we have been enabled again to reduce the weekly pay from the 1st April last to 8s. 9d. per week, and from the 1st October last to 8s. 6d. per week.

Your Committee reported last year a resolution to admit Private Patients, under certain regulations, at the same rate of pay as Pauper Patients, but at the same time stated their doubts whether the practice could be continued. The advantages to persons in humble life, not actually Paupers, was so manifest, that your Committee determined, notwithstanding the doubts they entertained, to give it a trial. We are now grieved to say that on account of the increase of

Pauper Patients in the Asylum, we have been compelled, for want of room, to discontinue receiving Private Patients.

Two of the Commissioners in Lunacy visited the Asylum on the 8th of May last, and made the following Report :—

(COPY REPORT.)

" Worcester County Lunatic Asylum,
" May 8th, 1858.

" There are 323 Patients in the Asylum (154 males and 169 females), 55 of whom appear to be under medical treatment. One Patient was secluded to-day. On reference to the Register, the instances of seclusion are rare. There has been only one case of restraint for the purpose of carrying into effect some surgical treatment. .

" Since the last visit of the Commissioners, on the 8th May, 1857, 131 Patients have been admitted, 38 have been discharged, and 30 have died ; the main causes of death being diseases of the brain and heart, paralysis, and epilepsy.

" We have to-day seen the Patients, and have inspected the wards, which are generally clean, and in very fair order. We think, however, that means should be at once taken to promote better ventilation in the ground-floor bed-rooms (single rooms), some of which are defective in this respect, owing to the difficulty of opening the windows."

" In reference to the points adverted to in the last entry, we learn—

" 1. That the Chapel is now in use.

" 2. That there is a Night Nurse for the females, who has no other employment than to walk out occasionally with some Patients, after three o'clock in the afternoon.

" There is no Night Nurse on the male side.

" 3. There is still no under-blanket allowed for the males.

" 4. One airing ground is planted, and another is sown and prepared for planting.

" 5. A walk of some extent has been made round the Asylum and its airing courts, and has been carried as far as the Gas-works ; but it is impracticable to take it round the estate, as suggested, owing to the brook which runs through the land and the inequalities of the ground.

" 6. No attempt has yet been made to improve the ventilation of the entrance-hall.

" 7. The Committee have authorized the admission of Private and Out-county Patients. There are now 3 Private Patients and 30 males from Bedford in the Asylum.

" In our progress through the Asylum we observed that some of the male dresses were wanting in neatness ; and we recommend that the Nurses and Attendants should be directed to employ a greater amount of towelling than appears to be the case at present, for the purpose of daily use.

" We enquired as to the number of Attendants and the wages paid to them. We think that the wages paid to the Female Attendants are below the sum usually paid in County Asylums, and scarcely enough to ensure good Nurses. The number of Nurses also is small, three of the wards, having respectively from 28 to 34 Patients, being provided with only one Nurse for each ward.

" Upon the whole we think the Asylum in very creditable condition, and under kind and careful superintendence.

" (Signed)

" B. W. PROCTOR, ⎞ *Commissioners*
" ROBERT NAIRNE, ⎠ *in Lunacy.*"

Your Committee took this Report into their consideration at the monthly meeting held on the 7th June last, and entered the following minutes in their order-book in reference thereto :—

(COPY.)

" With reference to the ventilation of the single bed-rooms, which Dr. Sherlock considers defective, it is ordered that Dr. Sherlock have a few of the windows altered as an experiment. With regard to the number of the Nurses, Dr. Sherlock considers them sufficient.

The average number at the present time is 1 Nurse to every 17 Patients.

"The Committee consider that the system now in use regulating the payment of wages here has given satisfaction to the Attendants, and are consequently of opinion that it does not require revision.

"The Committee think that the amount of wages paid to Attendants should be influenced to some extent by the amount of wages paid to ordinary domestic servants in the neighbourhood; and it appears, on comparison with other Asylums, that the wages here are above instead of below the average, as stated by the Commissioners.

"We do not consider that the other points mentioned by the Commissioners in their Report require any remark from the Committee, having all been adverted to by the Committee last year.

"We regret to find that the Commissioners made observations to some of the Nurses calculated to make them dissatisfied with the amount of their wages. The Committee think it would be better that any observations of the kind referred to should be made privately to Dr. Sherlock, or entered in the Report."

The Annual Report of 1857 shews that the number of Patients in the Asylum at the visit of the Sub-Committee on the 3rd December, prior to Epiphany Sessions, 1858, was 318, viz., 162 males and 156 females, including 30 males from Bedford County Asylum.

The Sub-Committee have visited the Asylum six times during the past year, and their reports as to the number of Patients is contained in the following table:—

1858.	MALES.	FEMALES.	TOTAL.
January 29th	158	160	318
April 8th	158	162	320
June 4th	157	172	329
July 30th	157	176	333
September 30th	162	180	342
December 3rd	163	184	347

B

The increase of the total number of Patients during the past year has been 29—28 females and 1 male. It will be seen that the fluctuation of number in regard to male Patients has been inconsiderable, whilst in reference to the females the number has been gradually and regularly increasing. The same observations as to males and females, in point of numbers, are applicable (to a small extent) to the year 1857. The last Annual Report (1857) shews that in December, 1856, the numbers were 115 males, 133 females—total, 248; and the numbers in December, 1857, had increased to 162 males, 156 females—total, 318; being an increase of 47 males and 23 females; but of the males, 30 were received from Bedford, so that the increase that year of this county and city Patients was 17 males and 23 females. We have deemed it necessary to draw attention to these facts for the two past years, and have no doubt they will be fully observed upon in the Report of the Medical Superintendent.

In consequence of the great increase of female Patients during the past year, we have had to provide much additional bedding and furniture at the expense of the county and city.

We regret to have to state that at the date of our visit on the 6th of December last, notwithstanding our additions, there were only four vacant beds on the female side of the building. We instituted enquiries, and found that temporary accommodation could be found, in case of emergency, for 15 additional beds; and this we propose to resort to if there should be occasion, rather than recommend any addition to the buildings; but it is clear that in case of the continued increase for another year to the same extent as the last, additional buildings must be erected. We annex to this Report a statement of the receipts and expenditure of money placed at our disposal by the county and city for repairs and furniture during the past year; and also a statement in regard to the mortgage debt.

In the present year we shall require the sum of £630, according to an estimate by Dr. Sherlock, for repairs and furniture. We therefore recommend the advance by the county of £560, and £70 by the city, to meet this.

Signed on behalf of the Committee,

T. G. CURTLER,

Chairman.

STATEMENT OF REPAIR AND FURNITURE ACCOUNT.

1858.	𝕽𝖊𝖈𝖊𝖎𝖕𝖙𝖘.	£.	s.	d.
Jan. 1.	By Balance from last account	8	4	2
April.	By Cash from County Treasurer, as per order of Court at last Epiphany Quarter Sessions, being the County's portion of £900	800	0	0
	By ditto of City Treasurer, City's portion of ditto	100	0	0
		£908	4	2

	𝕰𝖝𝖕𝖊𝖓𝖉𝖎𝖙𝖚𝖗𝖊.	£.	s.	d.
Mar. 1.	Paid George, balance account of Chapel drapery	4	0	6

GENERAL REPAIRS.

		£.	s.	d.			
Apl. 12.	Paid Russell and Sons for tubing	24	2	5			
	„ Perks for glass	6	12	5			
	„ Wood and Son for slates ...	2	11	0			
	„ Clare for lime	4	8	10			
	„ Jennings for water-closet ...	6	11	0			
	„ Hall for corrugated iron ...	6	7	1			
	„ Rowlands for slates and pipes	5	1	0			
	„ Bailey for gas retorts.........	13	12	9			
					69	6	6

MISCELLANEOUS.

	£.	s.	d.
Paid Rennington and Son, heating apparatus for Chapel	14	0	0
„ Carpenters' and Slaters' wages	29	2	6
Carried forward...........................	116	9	6

	£.	s.	d.
Brought forward	116	9	6

BEDDING AND FURNITURE.

	£.	s.	d.			
Paid Webb for horsehair	37	4	4			
„ Roddy for sheeting	93	8	0			
„ Norman for bedsteads	25	10	0			
„ Hemming for timber	21	11	10			
„ Turley and Co. for blankets and rugs	51	5	2			
„ Short and Son for birch wood	50	19	6			
				279	18	10

MISCELLANEOUS.

Paid Anderson for galvanic battery	4	7	6
„ Cox for gas regulator	16	10	0
„ Webb for garden drainage	35	3	1
June 7. „ Acock and Son for repairs and materials	15	10	9
„ R. Smith for shrubs and plants in airing courts	31	10	0

GENERAL REPAIRS.

Paid Hardy and Padmore for castings	5	16	9			
„ Hall for ironmongery	4	11	2			
„ Perks for paints	4	3	4			
„ Jones and Co. for nails, &c.	8	9	0			
„ Lingham for castors	4	7	6			
„ Williams for glass	2	17	9			
„ Bird for white lead, &c.	4	12	0			
„ Purslow for timber	4	8	1			
„ Eassie for ditto	41	0	9			
				80	6	4

Carried forward	579	16	0

	£.	s.	d.
Brought forward	579	16	0

	£.	s.	d.			
Paid Rowlands for fire-bricks, &c.	7	9	7			
„ Haden and Co. for castings	5	15	4			
„ Workmen's wages	24	10	0			
				37	14	11
„ Acock for bricks				6	15	0

BEDDING.

Paid Turley and Co. for blankets and rugs ....}	20	6	0			
„ Harker for seaweed	11	0	11			
„ Webb for horsehair	53	17	11			
				85	4	10
Sept. 6. „ Acock for lightning conductor				6	10	0

GENERAL REPAIRS.

Paid Richmond for repairs to mangle ....}	2	4	6			
„ Palmer and Co. for elm timber	2	12	8			
„ Short and Sons for veneers	4	0	10			
				8	18	0
Paid Rowlands and Sons for fire-bricks ....}	6	3	1			
„ Clare for lime..................	4	3	3			
„ Bird for oils and paints	12	12	6			
„ Anderson for ditto	6	19	3			
„ Hall for iron, &c.	8	19	6			
„ Bell and Hall for tools, &c.	5	10	5			
„ Workmen's wages	19	10	0			
„ Perks for anti-corrosive paint	7	10	0			
				71	8	0
Carried forward........................				796	6	9

	£.	s.	d.
Brought forward	796	6	9

	£.	s.	d.		£.	s.	d.
Oct. 9. Paid Davis for timber	56	0	0				
Less portion re-sold	40	11	9				
					15	8	3

	£.	s.	d.		£.	s.	d.
Dec. 6. Paid Walford and Hayes for repair to roads	14	18	6				
,, Lane and Bullock ditto	8	5	0				
,, Horton and Co. for scaffolding	2	9	11				
,, Anderson for oils, &c.	20	8	0				
,, Harrington and Co. for glaziers' tools	3	7	6				
,, Workmen's wages	20	15	10				
,, Mason for blinds	5	9	5				
,, Hall for iron	3	13	8				
,, Bird for paints	2	4	2				
					81	12	0
Balance in hand					14	17	2
					£908	4	2

STATEMENT IN REGARD TO MORTGAGE DEBT.

	FOR THE COUNTY.			CITY.			TOTAL.		
	£.	s.	d.	£.	s.	d.	£.	s.	d.
The total aggregate debt originally amounted to	56,888	17	8	7,111	2	4	64,000	0	0
Aggregate sums paid off	13,175	14	3	1,643	9	5	14,819	3	8
Balance now due	43,713	3	5	5,467	12	11	49,180	16	4

(Signed)   T. G. CURTLER.

General Results of each Year since the opening of the Asylum.

Dates.	Admitted.			Discharged.									Died.			Remained at close of year.			Average number resident.			Per centage of deaths on average number resident.			Per centage of recoveries on admissions.		
				Recovered.			Relieved.			Unimproved.																	
	Males.	Females.	Total.	Males.	Females.	Total.	Males.	Females.	Total.	Males.	Females.	Total.	Males.	Females.	Total.	Males.	Females.	Total.	Males.	Females.	Total.	Males.	Females.	Total.	Males.	Females.	Total.
From Aug. 11th to Dec. 31st, 1852	91	101	192	5	2	7	2	0	2	1	0	1	2	2	4	81	97	178	69	83	152	2.9	2.4	2.6	5.5	1.9	3.7
1853	52	45	97	9	16	25	2	3	5	1	2	3	19	12	31	102	109	211	90	104	194	21.1	11.5	16.3	17.3	35.5	26.4
1854	41	47	88	8	14	22	5	3	8	0	0	0	26	25	51	104	114	218	104	112	216	25.0	22.3	23.6	19.5	29.8	24.6
1855	53	48	101	19	19	38	7	5	12	0	0	0	24	15	39	107	123	230	110	121	231	21.8	12.4	17.1	35.8	39.6	37.7
1856	41	39	80	12	14	26	1	0	1	2	0	2	17	13	30	116	135	251	114	130	244	14.9	10.0	12.4	29.3	35.9	32.6
1857	74	56	130	18	11	29	2	0	2	3	0	3	10	19	29	157	161	318	124	149	273	8.0	12.7	10.3	24.8	19.6	22.2
1858	40	52	92	12	19	31	4	2	6	1	0	1	15	13	28	165	179	344	159	171	330	9.4	7.6	8.5	30.0	36.5	33.2
Totals	392	388	780	83	95	178	23	13	36	8	2	10	113	99	212				117	131	248	16.0	12.4	14.2	26.0	32.3	29.0

THE SIXTH ANNUAL REPORT

OF THE

MEDICAL SUPERINTENDENT.

To the Committee of Visitors of the County and City of Worcester Pauper Lunatic Asylum.

My Lord and Gentlemen,—There remained under treatment in the Asylum at the date of the last Annual Report 318 Patients, 157 males and 161 females. During the year 92 Patients, 40 males and 52 females, were admitted, making a total of 410 who have received the benefits of the Asylum. The admissions are 8 less than those of the preceding year, not taking into account the male Patients received under contract from the Bedford County Asylum. No case of readmission occurred during the year. The average number of admissions during the preceding five years, excluding those admitted at the opening of the Asylum from their several places of residence, was 93, so that the number received during the present year is as near the average as possible, and may be taken as a guide in estimating the probable requirements of the county and city for future years. For purposes of reference is subjoined a Table showing the results of the several years since the opening of the Asylum, including the present year. The average number of Patients resident in the Asylum during the past year was 330—an

c

advance of 57 on the preceding year—caused in great measure amongst the males by the presence of the out-county Patients, and amongst the females by a much lower mortality than usual; and by the advanced character of insanity not admitting of recovery in many of the admissions, only 12 of those admitted having been discharged recovered. Amongst those received during the year and presenting but little prospect of recovery were 5 Patients with congenital defect of mind, 3 more of the same class associated with epilepsy; there were 8 suffering from epilepsy, 6 from general paralysis, and 1 from hemiphlegia; 5 were in a state of great danger, or dying; and in 14 the duration of their insanity varied from two to nearly thirty years—in all 42 persons, or 46 per cent. of the total admissions. Such an enumeration clearly shows that there still exists in this county a large amount of mental disease still not under care and treatment in an Asylum, and the attention of Boards of Guardians, and of their Medical and Relieving Officers, cannot be too often or urgently directed to the placing of such cases under treatment while a reasonable expectation of their recovery still exists. The indication or infliction of violence upon themselves or others, the degree of their helplessness, bodily disease, and uncleanliness of habits, should not alone be permitted to suggest the propriety of the removal of a Patient to the Asylum a few weeks or months before death may be anticipated; nor should their noise and destruction of property be the only criterion adopted, and then not with regard to their recovery, but as a means of securing tranquillity and discipline in the Union, and saving furniture and clothing from being injured. Undoubtedly many of the inmates of an Asylum in some stage of their illness have presented such psychological peculiarities which have rendered their admission necessary, but there are other large classes of the insane who present none of these, and are still equally benefited by treatment and residence in an Asylum, and if neglected and allowed to vegetate at home or in a Workhouse, they pass into a worse form of the disease, and ultimately die in a state of mental alienation. Such are many Patients suffering from dementia, melancholia, monomania, and mania, who are quiet in their demeanour and habits, and endure without complaint any amount of want of care and treatment, while their mental disease is making great progress, and destroying the power of their intellect. In every well-conducted Asylum it should be borne in mind that the attention and skill of the Physician and his Attendants are required equally often and seriously by those of the latter class of Patients as by the former. Of the admissions 55 were cases of the first attack of insanity, 20 of the second, and 5 of the third; while 10 others were reported as having experienced several attacks, but their number was not ascertained.

As regards their social condition, 52 were unmarried or widowed, and 38 were married: as is usual, a greater immunity from the disease prevails amongst those of the latter class. Only rather above 8 per cent. of the cases had received a good common education; 29 per cent. were able to read and write, and had received some rudimentary education; 38 per cent. were only sufficiently educated to be able to read; 15 per cent. were known to have received not the least instruction; and in above rather 8 per cent. more no information could be gathered on the subject from any source. In the reported cases 47 per cent. were members of the Established Church, 32 per cent. were Protestant Dissenters of various denominations, 17 per cent. were Methodists, and only a few examples of persons of other religious persuasions were admitted.

The ages of the Patients admitted, and discharged cured, are given in Table XIII., which shows that by far the largest proportion of the attacks occur to persons in the middle periods of life, after the mind has attained to its full power and capacity, and when it is more completely occupied with the cares and distracting anxieties of life, and that the ratio of seizures subsequently declines with each advance of life. It appears from the same Table that as regards the males a larger number of cases, viz., 11, were admitted in the decennial period between 50 and 60, but on examining the individual cases it is found that some of this age have been idiotic from birth, others have had two or more attacks of insanity previously, or have been in a state of insanity for many years, all of which causes render their appearance in this division exceptional, and does not favour the presumption of a greater liability to an attack at this period of life. As a general rule it may be stated that the chances of recovery after arriving at puberty are greatest in proportion to the youth of the Patient, and that these diminish with each advance of life. The excess of recoveries as regards the males from 50 to 60 years of age is, as in the former case, to be ascribed to the recurrent character of the insanity in three at least of the persons who recovered at that age.

The 12th Table is instructive in pointing out that 28 of the 31 Patients who were discharged recovered had been placed under treatment within twelve months of the appearance of their insanity. If any one fact deserves attention in regulating the conduct of those having the control of Patients in the early stage of their illness, it is the urgent importance of placing them under treatment at once, on the nature of their illness becoming manifest.

The recoveries, calculated upon the total admissions, was at the rate of 33.7 per cent. for both sexes : for the males it was at the rate of 30 per cent., and for the females at the rate of 36.5 per cent. Recoveries are generally more numerous in the female sex, from the comparative absence in them of diseases of the brain, complicated with paralysis. It has already been stated that in 42 of the admissions there was at the time of their entering the Asylum no prospect, however remote, of their insanity terminating in recovery ; and excluding these from the calculations, the ratio of recovery upon those probably curable was 62 per cent.

Seven Patients left the Asylum in a state of incomplete recovery, of whom 5 were transferred to other Institutions in consequence of changes in their settlements, 1 was taken in charge by her friends, and 1 was discharged after escaping and remaining concealed beyond the time when he could be re-taken. He has since been heard of as having obtained work in the neighbourhood, and as no application has been made for his re-admission, he is probably doing well.

The mortality is at the rate of 8.5 per cent., calculated upon the average number of Patients resident throughout the year : 9.4 per cent. for the males, and 7.6 per cent. for the females—the proportion which usually prevails as regards the sexes is here present. This ratio is 2 per cent. lower than that of the previous year, and may be considered favourable : it is lower than that of any previous year since the opening of the Asylum. The ages of two persons deceased varied from 60 to 70, of two from 70 to 80, and one woman had attained to the age of 92 years. One Patient survived his admission less than 24 hours ; he had been much exhausted from abstinence and depressing mental emotions, and died in consequence. One female died within one week, one within two, and another within six ; in all, seven persons died within three months of their admission, a fourth of the total mortality of the year.

Inquests were held in three cases of death during the year. One was that of an epileptic female, who died in a fit during the night, and was found dead in bed by the Night-nurse in the course of her visitations. The second was that of a man, who died on the morning of the day following his admission from exhaustion, the result of extreme mental depression and of almost constant refusal of food during an illness of some two months previous duration. The third was in that of a male Patient, who succeeded in escaping from the house when other Patients were entering it after the completion of their day's work, and although missed immediately, and pursued by several Attendants, was not successfully tracked. In going to Worcester through the fields (probably to avoid detection) he struck the river Teme, then in a state of flood, and divesting himself of his clothing, entered it, either for the purpose of crossing it more securely or of committing suicide. His body was found in the river the following day, attention being attracted to the place by the clothing found on the bank. Verdicts were given in each case in accordance with the above evidence. Such occurrences as the latter, which necessarily cast a gloom over the Asylum, and are attended with much distress and anxiety, cannot always be avoided; and considering the number of persons constantly under treatment having impulses of a dangerous character, over whom almost constant supervision must be for long periods maintained, it is satisfactory to know that only one other instance of accidental death has occurred in the Asylum since its opening. The amount of personal liberty which is now generally accorded to most Patients in Asylums renders their occasional escape not unfrequent, and much greater injury to the majority would result from establishing such a strict code of regulations as would render such a contingency impossible. When it is remembered that about three-fourths of the total male Patients are for the most part employed about the premises on any given day, it will be evident that chances of escape are continually offered, and the unfrequency with which this privilege is taken advantage of renders us desirous of extending the freedom of their movements within our boundaries as much as is possibly consistent with their safety, treatment, and proper supervision.

Nine deaths resulted from general paralysis, in two of whom there was present maniacal excitement and great restlessness, favouring the fatal termination by inducing exhaustion early in the course of the disease; in four others it had attained an advanced stage, and was attended with sloughing of the surface and colliquative diarrhœa. Meningitis was fatal in one case, cerebral congestion in another, to which was superadded pneumonia during the course of its progress. One died suddenly of epilepsy during the fit; a second also suddenly, after the fit, in whom there was extensive heart disease; and a third during the epileptic convulsions, in whom was found an extensive rupture of the spleen, which organ was in an advanced stage of disease. Fourteen deaths were thus connected with disease of the brain or other central nervous masses. Six deaths resulted from gradual wearing out of the system, in two of whom there existed a diseased repugnance to food, with extreme mental distress, or excitement with delusions; a third, with extensive disease of the mesenteric glands and high maniacal excitement of long duration; a fourth, with co-existent spinal and liver disease, which encroached upon the space occupied by the lungs, and was accompanied by furious maniacal delirium; and the two last from the decay of old age, with bronchitis and asthma. One death resulted from asphyxia by drowning, 1 from disease of the suprarenal capsules, 1 from phlebitis, consequent upon inflammation of the hand, and occurring in a person suffering from disease of the kidneys; 1 from gastro-enteritis, and 4 from phthisis and its usual complications. Of the 24 cases in which an examination was made during the year, the following are the chief pathological appearances observed in the encephalon :—Increased density and thickness of the cranium were remarked in 11 instances : in 2 of acute mania, in 1 of epileptic mania, in 1 of melancholia, in 2 of dementia, and in 5 of general paralysis. The dura mater had formed abnormal adhesions to the cranium or arachnoid in 11 instances : in 4 of general paralysis, in 1 of acute mania, in 1 of mania with epilepsy, in 1 of melancholia, in 2 of dementia, in 1 of dementia with epilepsy, and in 1 of chronic mania. Congestion of the membranes and of the substance of the brain was present in 8 : in 2 of general paralysis, in 2 of acute mania, in 1 of mania with epilepsy, in 1 of dementia, in 1 of chronic mania, and in 1 of melancholia. An opposite or exsanguine condition of the same parts was noticed in 9 : in 2 of general paralysis, in 1 of mania with epilepsy, in 1 of dementia, in 1 of dementia with epilepsy, in 1 of chronic mania, in 1 of monomania, in 1 of idiotcy, and in 1 of hysteric mania; these were cases of persons dying of various exhausting diseases at an advanced stage of their progress. The arachnoid was thickened, opaque, and more or less adherent in 21 instances: in 6 of general paralysis, in 3 of acute mania, in 1 of mania with epilepsy, in 3 of dementia, in 2 of monomania, in 3 of chronic mania, in 1 of dementia with epilepsy, in 1 of idiotcy, and in 1 of hysteric mania. The membranes adhered to the cortical grey substance in 4 cases: in 3 of general paralysis and in 1 of acute mania. The substance of the brain was softer than natural in 9 cases: in 1 of acute mania, in 2 of epileptic mania, in 1 of general paralysis, in 1 of dementia, in 1 of chronic mania, in 1 of monomania, in 1 of idiotcy, and in 1 of hysteric mania. The cortical grey substance was much softened in 10 instances : in 6 of general paralysis, in 1 of acute mania, in 1 of melancholia, in 1 of chronic mania, and 1 of dementia with epilepsy. The lining of the lateral and other ventricles was found having a frosted or minutely granular appearance in 6 cases : in 5 of general paralysis and in 1 of acute mania. Atheromatous or osseous deposits were seen in the coats of the cerebral vessels in 4 instances : in 2 of general paralysis, in 1 of dementia, and in 1 of monomania. Effusion of serous or sero-sanguinolent fluid had occurred into the texture of the pia mater and into the sac of the arachnoid in 17 instances : in 7 of general paralysis, in 1 of acute mania, in 1 of epileptic mania, in 1 of dementia, in 1 of melancholia, in 3 of chronic mania, in 2 of mono-mania, and in 1 of dementia with epilepsy. A large accumulation of serous fluid was found in the ventricles of 11 cases: in 2 of acute mania, in 1 of chronic mania, in 1 of dementia, in 1 of dementia with epilepsy, in 1 of monomania, and in 5 of general paralysis. The convolutions were diminished in size in a very marked degree in 1 case of senile dementia, in 1 of monomania, and in 1 of chronic mania. In 1 case of melancholia, a recent effusion of blood was found over the hemispheres beneath the dura mater. A false membrane was found over the parts corresponding with the circle of Willis in 1 case of general paralysis. A spicula of bone (pea size) was observed in the falx cerebri of 1 case of chronic mania, of many years standing. In 1 case of general paralysis, bony plates were present on either side of the central ridge of the frontal bone. Forty-three of the cases admitted

D

presented a suicidal tendency, in the proportion of 46 per cent. of all who entered the Asylum. About equal numbers had made actual attempts upon their lives, and had meditated the infliction of such injury upon themselves. This ratio is much larger than that observed heretofore, but the severity of the impulse (with a few exceptions) has been less grave and more amenable to treatment. In cases of melancholia and mania the disposition was more frequently developed than in other forms of insanity. In most of the females there was present severe constitutional disturbance and debility, the result of long-continued bad health, and of care and various other depressing emotions of the mind ; while in looking over the list of the males presenting this peculiarity more powerful passions, reverses, losses, anxiety, and emotions of greater intensity were generally observed to be in operation, with subsequent deterioration of the bodily health.

In Table VI. is enumerated the causes of the mental disease of the admissions of the year, so far as they could be gleaned from the parochial authorities or the friends of the Patients who subsequently visited them. In 79 cases some cause or combination of circumstances was ascertained to have preceded the attack, and appeared to the persons having the care of the Patients to have influenced and changed the normal current and coherence of their thoughts, their character, disposition, and habits. In 58 per cent. of the total ascertained cases (63 per cent. for the males and 54 per cent. for the females) the causes were of a physical character ; and in 42 per cent. (36 per cent. as regards the males and 45 per cent. of the females) the causes appeared to be of a moral or mental character. In both series, however, some cases presented a combination rendering it difficult if not impossible to assign the case with certainty to one class rather than to the other; but the selection was given in favour of that agency which immediately preceded the attack, and not to the one which had induced a state of mind or habit of body favourable for its action or occurrence. Insanity the result of physical causes is thus 16 per cent. more prevalent than that induced by moral influences. In many districts of the country the reverse of this prevails; but, as is usually found here, the male admissions from these causes are much more numerous than the female. Fevers, erysipelas, childbirth, dentition, epilepsy, uterine disease and irritation, spinal disease, falls and injuries to the head, intemperance, excesses of various kinds, previous attacks of insanity, and the predisposition to it transmitted from parents, congenital malformation or arrested cerebral development, feeble and diseased states of the system, overtaxing the bodily powers, cerebral atrophy, food insufficient or of bad quality, are the chief physical causes observed, of which intemperance and its concomitant evils account for over 17 per cent. of the cases in this division, or for above 10 per cent. of the cases whose history has been learned. Among the chief moral causes enumerated may be mentioned—remorse at committing murder during a poaching affray, fright at losing friends in a large and populous city, or at seeing friends suddenly killed or mutilated during colliery accidents, seduction and disappointment of the affections, desertion of the husband or wife, domestic quarrels and differences, difficulties, reverses and losses of various kinds, want of employment, anxiety and distress of mind from various sources, and protracted nursing and attendance on friends in a state of suffering and illness.

The health and condition of the Inmates has been unusually satisfactory during the year, the mortality much lower than the average, and the recoveries in their usual proportion. No disease of an epidemic character has prevailed, and there has been less than the usual amount of casual illness. Simultaneously with changes in the seasons, there have been exacerbations in the mental illness of many of the Patients, especially of such as suffer from epilepsy and paralysis, severe and numerous cases of which diseases generally occur both among the male and female population, and are probably due to some unexplained changes in the condition and temperature of the atmosphere. The above statement is valuable as exhibiting the sanatary condition of the Asylum in a favourable point of view, and in proving the excellence of the site selected for the purpose of the Asylum in this respect; especially if the condition of the Patients at the time of their admission, as shown in Table XVII., is examined, which states that 69 per cent. of them were then in a bad or indifferent state of health from the various causes there set forth.

The treatment of the Patients continues to be conducted on the same principles as have previously been enunciated in former Reports : while the utmost amount of liberty consistent with each individual's case is accorded, both as regards their amusements, occupations, and freedom of movement within the Asylum boundaries, yet they are still subject to daily medical supervision, and the constant watchfulness of Attendants, who carry out the instructions and details of moral treatment adapted to the case of each. Very many cases require medical treatment and a careful regimen, from the presence of active bodily disease. Diseases attended with derangements of nutrition require constant attention : numbers are daily supplied with stimulants and other medical comforts as the only means of insuring their recovery and promoting improvement in their health and condition, owing to the low, feeble, and emaciated state in which they may be sent to the

Asylum or to which they may be reduced by the progress, severity, and continuance of their mental disease. The complication of insanity with diseased states of the heart, lungs, liver, and stomach, in addition to those affecting the brain or its membranes, are often met with, and occasion much of the mortality of the Asylum. Granular degeneration of the kidney, said to be infrequent amongst the insane in some counties, is here not unusual, and numerous cases of diseased kidneys are found on examination and are recognised during life but there is generally observed an absence of dropsy, of albuminous urine, and other symptoms which are for the most part expected to be present during its course. The occurrence of gradually increasing coma from poisoning of the blood and convulsions have not, however, unfrequently disclosed the nature of such a case towards its last stages. Rheumatism and gouty formations, with diseased conditions of the cerebral and other vessels, leading to defective nutrition of the brain, and interfering with a proper supply of blood, are often present. Uterine diseases are often met with, associated with the mental disease of females at the time of puberty, and also at the climacteric period of life. Various forms of paralysis, of epilepsy, and many diseased conditions of the brain, especially in their advanced stages, are always under treatment in every Asylum, and increase their mortality in proportion to their frequency of occurrence.

Various Tables, as usual, accompany this Report which indicate the amount of activity, nature, and extent of employment afforded for the male and female Patients. The lists of work executed show a degree of praiseworthy exertion, beneficial both to those employed therein as also to those having the immediate direction of those several departments. The various trades are beginning to acquire a solidity and permanence which were once thought impossible, from the absence of skilled artisans amongst the Patients, but the continued exertions of the Attendants have gradually established a class of expert workers in each trade from those labouring under chronic insanity whose labour is now becoming valuable and profitable. A large proportion of the men are still employed in the various agricultural pursuits connected with the farm and garden, while others less manageable and expert are occupied in levelling, making roads, and other heavy earthworks, in which considerable progress has been made during the year. The females are employed for the most part in the laundry, kitchen, and in assisting the Attendants, and also in the making and repairing of the clothing used in the Asylum. Various minor additions have been made to the comforts and accommodation of the Patients, and also several useful works executed in connection with the domestic economy and efficiency of the Asylum. Additions have been made to the accommodation at the expense of the materials used, whereby 40 more Patients can be received than were resident at the opening of the year. Wardrobes have been added where required, and several have been enlarged ; the library has been fitted up ; 20 dozens of pictures have been framed and glazed ; the washing machine has been remade ; chests of drawers, work and dining tables, settees, ottomans, easy chairs, some dressing tables, and clothes boxes, have been added to the furniture, especially in the female wards. The male hospital has been painted in oil colours and in part grained, as also the kitchen, several bath-rooms, and lavatories, to avoid damp and the retention and condensation of escaped steam upon the walls. The new Chapel has been provided with a hot-air apparatus ; the oven has been rebuilt and enlarged to meet the expansion of the Asylum ; fire-guards have been made for the open fires in the dormitories of the new galleries; two retorts have been fixed at the gas-works to replace others worn out, and the gasometer has been painted and repaired. It is an agreeable duty to report that the comfort, happiness, and tranquillity of the Patients are materially benefited by these improvements, and that extensive destruction of property or clothing are extremely rare, excepting amongst recent acute cases or persons with chronic insanity who have been neglected and only recently received into the Asylum. To promote and secure the tranquillity and contentment of those labouring under mental disease is one great step towards their recovery, forasmuch as much decided benefit and relief cannot be expected to occur while they remain in an irritable, restless, and dissatisfied state of mind. The associations are more natural under these circumstances, and they are less reminded of their removal from their homes and friends: they experience less bodily discomfort, and those whose home the Asylum is for life regard the change with less annoyance and feelings of irritation.

Classified walking parties continue to take exercise in the grounds and neighbouring country, according as the state of their minds admit of one or the other privilege, especially during the spring, summer, and autumn. Excursions of Patients of either sex are permitted at intervals to spend a day in some favourite locality, and small parties are occasionally sent to Worcester to attend a concert or other place of amusement. Single Patients almost daily visit their friends, appreciate the indulgence, and acquire confidence in the Asylum and their treatment. A singing class assembles two evenings each week for the practice of sacred music and glee singing. Weekly and illustrated periodicals and the books of the library are circulated through the several galleries, and those able to read are encouraged to do so in the evenings, the Attendants performing this duty for them when a substitute cannot be found. The weekly parties for music, dancing, and acting of light comedy are still in the greatest favour, and appear beneficial by bringing together the Patients of both sexes under the observation of the Officers, thereby favouring self-control and improvements in their manners, tastes, dress, and habits.

The preponderance of the female Patients, which was more fully discussed in the last Report, still continues, but to a less degree; and should the same prevail in an equal ratio during the ensuing year, it is presumed that a further increase of accommodation in that department will be required. At present the Asylum, as now arranged, is nearly full as regards this sex, but by the adoption of temporary arrangements in various situations provision can be made for the admission of the probable increase of another year, but beyond that date it is probable that female Patients can only be received as recoveries or deaths may occasion a vacancy.

Twenty-six persons of those admitted were occupied in connection with agriculture, or at the rate of 31 per cent. of the total admissions pursuing some calling; 39 were engaged in personal service in trade or in mechanical arts, or 46 per cent. of those having known occupations; 15 were engaged in manufacture, or 17 per cent. of the same class; and 5 were employed in works connected with minerals or mining, or at the rate of 6 per cent. calculated in the same way.

Both in this and other counties much anxiety and discussion have arisen in consequence of the expressed opinion that insanity is greatly on the increase, for this and other Asylums have since their establishment been filled with Patients, and in most instances enlarged; and the annual returns furnished to the Visiting Justices, Commissioners in Lunacy, and the Poor Law Board exhibit a progressive increase in the number of

Patients chargeable to the several Unions, and favour a similar conclusion. If this statement and such statistics, which are correct (so far as they go), were alone taken into account, the result would be, as stated, a positive increase of insanity; but on enquiring into the subject it is found that the facts do not warrant such a conclusion. At any given date, even up to the present time, there are no returns in existence which show the number of actual lunatics and idiots in any district of the country, but only such as are chargeable to their parishes, or are confined in private Asylums, or are under certificate as single Patients are known and enumerated in the published returns. Chancery lunatics, and all those of unsound mind under the care of their friends in their own houses or lodgings, and not kept for profit, are unknown so far as statistics are concerned. Pauper lunacy is each year largely recruited from the latter class of Patients, owing in great measure to the want of proper Asylums for the middle class and for that class immediately above the rank of paupers. There are thus no data from which to calculate, and it appears extremely desirable that in the approaching census steps should be taken to clear up this difficulty by a series of well-defined enquiries into the mental condition of each member of the community; thus a starting point would be obtained for the settlement of this important question. There are several considerations which tend to show an apparent increase of insanity. Many persons are now deemed insane and fit objects for Asylum care and treatment who a few years ago were called "flighty," " soft," or " peculiar," and it is thought that many such are still at large. Many cases of maniacal dilirium from various causes, of mania with brain disease, and of the impairment of mind consequent on old age, and of congenital mental weakness, find their

F

way into Asylums, and who were formerly never sent thereto. Asylums were then regarded, and often justly, as places where persons of the most ferocious violence were by main force and restraint of the severest character prevented from following their impulses, and the means by which this was accomplished were either unknown or frequently (if discovered) were of a brutal and degrading character. But few recovered, many died mysteriously and suddenly, none gave them care or protection or deemed them capable of receiving sympathy or of deriving benefit from kind words and treatment, and such reports as did appear of their management led eyery one to avoid them. Friends therefore never applied for the admission of their relatives into them, but each unfortunate Patient, if at all manageable by fetters and confinement, was kept at home and treated according to the disposition and judgment of those in whose care they were. Now from changes in the constitution and management of Asylums, and a gradually extending confidence in their usefulness, Patients' friends, sooner or later, take steps for the removal of the majority of such cases to some Asylum, and only a few Patients suffering from severe forms of insanity are occasionally brought to light as receiving neglect or cruel treatment under the hands of their friends at home. However, that unreported and unrecognised cases exist in considerable numbers throughout the country, the frequency of suicides, of assaults, and various crimes committed by persons of unsound mind, and reported in the various journals and daily papers as coming under the notice of courts of justice, clearly establish. That such feelings have an influence upon the admissions into our Asylums is also clearly shown by the apparently great increase of insanity which is observed to occur in every place after the opening of a well-regulated Asylum for their care and recovery. Public attention has also of late years been more fully directed to the diseased conditions of mind, and a band of men, zealous for the amelioration and care of such as are afflicted with insanity, have grown up, superintended by Visiting Justices, Commissioners in Lunacy, and other safeguards against abuse of power and cruelty, the result of which has been the means of accumulating in Asylums a great proportion of the existing lunatics, and certainly with great benefit to the sufferers. There is but little doubt but that the founding and opening of Asylums for the middle classes of society would greatly add to the perfection of our existing machinery for the care and recovery of the insane. This is proved by the not unfrequent applications made for the reception of such persons into the present County and Borough Asylums by their friends. They have confidence in their management, and would in many cases forego the objection to their friends associating with persons in a lower state of society than themselves in order that they may receive the benefits to be derived from them. Some persons of this rank impoverish themselves by the payment of larger rates of board than they can afford for their care in private and licensed houses, and others are detained at home under the care and charge of their friends, where they probably become incurable. It should always be remembered that the great remedy for the decrease of insanity would be the recovery of every one seized with it. To enable experts to accomplish this early treatment must be had recourse to, which in from 60 to nearly 80 per cent. of such cases would be successful. Rather less than 10 per cent. of such cases would die under treatment, and from 10 to 20 per cent. would only remain in a chronic state of insanity. It now unfortunately happens in most of our large Asylums, from the non-observance of these rules, that the proportions of the incurables or chronic insane, and of those recovered, are the reverse of that already stated, and this altogether from delay in their treatment. This is the one great feeder of the insanity of the country. The duration of life amongst the insane is now considerably prolonged, owing to the increased care, comfort, and attention bestowed upon them, which would favour a larger number of them being alive at any given date. It is probable that some of the insanity and idiotcy of the country could be prevented by the exercise of greater care in forming marriage connections, a subject difficult to deal with but deserving of the greatest attention and consideration. Marriages of relatives should be avoided as certain to concentrate and intensify the disposition to insanity, which may exist in any family, and persisted in for some generations would produce and foster the disposition, if not already acquired. The marriages of persons of weak and imbecile minds should be guarded against in every possible way. It unfortunately happens that such persons are generally the most prone to marry early, disregarding the terrible consequences to their offspring. Amongst the poor it would be preferable to maintain such persons, who generally incline to lead a wandering and vagrant life, and are of naturally weak mind, under constant care and supervision, rather than have at intervals to hear of their seduction and of their having given birth to one or more children, who are all certain to become chargeable for life to their parishes, and be deficient both in mental and bodily development.

The following Table gives the population in 1851 of the 11 Unions comprised in the county and city of Worcester, excluding from observation several Unions, portions of which are connected to those of other counties; the second column gives the number of lunatics, idiots, and insane persons returned as chargeable to each on the 1st January, 1859; the third column gives the number of the same under care and treatment in the Asylum; and the two last columns the rates which these bear to the general population of 1851—the last census :—

Names of Unions.	Population according to Census of 1851.	No. of Lunatics, Idiots, &c., chargeable to Unions on 1st Jany, 1859.	No. of Lunatics, Idiots, &c., in Asylum on 1st Jany., 1859.	Ratio of Lunatics, Idiots, and Insane to the population in 1851.	Ratio of Lunatics, Idiots, and Insane in Asylum, on 1st Jany, 1859, to the population of 1851.
Stourbridge	57,350	33	22	1 in 1738	1 in 2,607
Kidderminster	32,917	66	38	„ „ 499	„ „ 866
Tenbury	7,047	9	4	„ „ 783	„ „ 1,762
Martley	13,791	32	12	„ „ 431	„ „ 1,149
Worcester	27,237	66	58	„ „ 412	„ „ 469
Upton-on-Severn	18,070	46	22	„ „ 393	„ „ 821
Evesham	14,463	20	12	„ „ 723	„ „ 1,205
Pershore	13,553	24	21	„ „ 564	„ „ 645
Droitwich	18,023	35	16	„ „ 515	„ „ 1,126
Bromsgrove	24,822	48	19	„ „ 517	„ „ 1,306
Kings's Norton	30,871	22	19	„ „1403	„ „ 1,625
	258,144	401	243	1 in 644	1 in 1,062
England and Wales	17,927,000	36,249	22,911	„ „ 494	„ „ 782

For facility of reference and the purpose of comparison the population of England and Wales is given according to the census of 1851, and the numbers of lunatics, idiots, and insane persons on 1st January, 1859, reported by the Commissioners in Lunacy, as existing in Asylums of all sorts, military hospitals, single patients under certificate, and those confined in Workhouses and boarded with relatives or strangers, is also given; and also the number of Patients of the same class then in Asylums. On looking over this Table it is at once observed that the proportion of insane in this county and city are, taking the Unions together, much below the average of

England and Wales, and this as regards both the known cases of insanity and also those under care in the Asylum. Did the same proportions prevail in this county and city as are returned for England and Wales, the numbers of the insane would amount to 522 for the portion included in the Table, and 330 would be the number resident in the Asylum, both much larger than the actual figures. It does not appear manifest why Upton-on-Severn Union should have a larger proportion of lunacy than any other in the county, excepting it be presumed that from its proximity to the Asylum the cases are sooner recognised and entered in the returns under their proper name. The Worcester Union also, in close proximity to the Asylum, displays a large amount of mental disease; and as a general rule, as we recede from the Asylum, the ratio of the insane decreases. It has never been suggested that the presence of an Asylum in a given district causes insanity, but it certainly ensures greater accuracy in the returns, and induces friends and relations of persons afflicted to apply for their admission, thus raising the ratio to a great extent in its immediate neighbourhood. It may be stated that cases of mental unsoundness occurring amongst the poor of our neighbourhood are from time to time heard of who never enter the Asylum, so that even in the district immediately surrounding we have no accurate data for calculations. The Stourbridge and Kings Norton Unions are extremely low in their returns, but it is not probable that they enjoy a greater immunity from insanity than Worcester or Upton-on-Severn; indeed, considering the character of the mass of their population, there might be anticipated a larger ratio from those districts. The greatest difference also is observed to prevail as regards the proportion which the known cases bear to those in the Asylum. Worcester sends 58 out of 66, Kidderminster 38 out of the same number, Bromsgrove 19 out of 48, and so on. No variety in the character of their insanity can account for this vast discrepancy; but ideas of fancied economy are probably the source of the diversity of practice which prevails. In connection with this subject it may be stated that the accounts of Asylums and of Unions are kept on different systems, so that no comparison can be drawn as to the expense of a lunatic in one or the other place from the amount of payments made at either. In Asylums all are adults and full grown, consuming the full allowance of food of an able-bodied man; in Workhouses there is a large proportion of children, of infants in arms, and others on a less scale of diet. All establishment charges are included in the payment made by the parish to the Asylum, while in the Union these are defrayed from a different source. The cost of a lunatic in a Workhouse is calculated on averages, including infants and children, and only takes in clothing; while in an Asylum everything is included in the charge. On calculating these particulars, and having regard to the destruction and trouble occasioned by the presence of idiots and lunatics in a Workhouse, and their manifest unfitness for such care, it will be found that the rate of charge is, if anything, lower in the Asylum than in the Union, regard being had to the nature of the diet and accessories requisite for such persons due care.

Thanking the Committee of Visitors for their continued confidence and support, and for their attention to all matters submitted for their consideration, I have the honour to submit this, the Sixth Report of the Asylum.

JAMES SHERLOCK.

To the Committee of Visitors of the Worcester County and City Pauper Lunatic Asylum.

MY LORD AND GENTLEMEN,—Without entering into details, which would perhaps be out of place in a Report of this kind, I have great satisfaction in being able to assure you, after some years experience of my present charge, that I consider my ministrations here as acceptable, and probably as beneficial as they might be among an ordinary congregation of sane persons. There are many in the Asylum, I am sure, who find their church a comfort and a blessing to them ; and of those who have been removed by death, there have been some of whose religious state I could not but entertain the most favourable opinion.

I have also reason to know that some of the Patients who have left the Asylum "cured" retain a grateful remembrance of the religious advantages which they enjoyed here. I cannot conclude without thanking you, my Lord and Gentlemen, for the liberal supply of Bibles and Prayer Books, which has enabled me to present a copy to each of every discharged Patient requiring them.

I am, my Lord and Gentlemen,

Your faithful Servant,

E. HORTON,

CHAPLAIN.

TABLE I.—*General Results of the Year.*

	Males.	Females.	Total.
Number of Inmates at close of 1857...	157	161	318
Admitted during the year 1858 ...	40	52	92
Total under treatment	197	213	410
 M. F. T. Discharged ... 17 21—38 M. F. T. Of whom were Cured ... 12 19—31 „ „ Relieved.. 4 2— 6 „ „ Unimproved 1 0— 1 Died ... ... 15 13—28			
(Died row totals)	32	34	66
Number of Inmates at close of 1858...	165	179	344
Average number resident throughout } the year ... ...}	159	171	330

TABLE II.—*Showing the number of Admissions, Discharges, and Deaths, in each Month.*

	ADMISSIONS.			DISCHARGES.			DEATHS.		
	Males.	Females.	Total.	Males.	Females.	Total.	Males.	Females.	Total.
January	3	3	6	1	3	4	0	1	1
February	2	4	6	1	1	2	2	2	4
March	3	3	6	3	0	3	0	2	2
April	3	10	13	2	2	4	4	1	5
May	4	5	9	2	2	4	0	0	0
June	3	6	9	1	2	3	1	0	1
July	2	1	3	0	1	1	3	0	3
August	5	5	10	0	1	1	1	1	2
September	1	4	5	0	1	1	0	2	2
October	3	7	10	3	3	6	2	1	3
November	5	3	8	1	0	1	2	2	4
December	6	1	7	3	5	8	0	1	1
Total	40	52	92	17	21	38	15	13	28

G

42

TABLE III.—*Form of Mental Disease in those admitted.*

	Males.	Females.	Total.
Mania, Acute	10	13	23
„ Chronic	1	8	9
„ Recurrent	2	2	4
„ Hysteric	0	2	2
„ Puerperal	0	1	1
„ with Epilepsy	5	2	7
„ „ General Paralysis ...	5	0	5
Dementia	3	8	11
„ Senile	0	1	1
„ with Paralysis	0	1	1
„ „ General Paralysis ...	1	0	1
„ „ Hysteric Epilepsy ...	0	1	1
Melancholia	4	6	10
Monomania of Suspicion	1	1	2
„ of Fear	2	1	3
„ of Unseen Agency ...	0	2	2
„ of Superstition	1	0	1
Amentia	4	1	5
„ with Epilepsy	1	2	3
Total	40	52	92

TABLE IV.—*Duration of Disease in those admitted.*

	Males.	Females.	Total.
Under 1 month	14	17	31
„ 3 months	5	8	13
„ 6 „	2	7	9
„ 9 „	1	4	5
„ 12 „	1	1	2
Above 1 year	1	1	2
„ 2 years	2	2	4
„ 3 „	1	3	4
„ 6 „	1	0	1
„ 7 „	1	1	2
„ 9 „	1	0	1
„ 10 „	0	1	1
„ 14 „	0	1	1
„ 24 „	0	1	1
For years (undefined)	3	0	3
From birth	5	3	8
Unknown	2	2	4
Total	40	52	92

TABLE V.—*Showing the Number of Attacks of Insanity in the Admissions of the Year.*

	Males.	Females.	Total.
Cases of first attack	22	33	55
„ second „	8	12	20
„ third „	3	2	5
Have had several attacks	6	4	10
Unknown	1	1	2
Total	40	52	92

44

TABLE VI.—*Assigned Causes of Disease in those admitted.*

	Males.	Females.	Total.
Fever	1	1	2
,, and Erysipelas of Head	0	1	1
Epilepsy	2	2	4
Dentition	0	1	1
Suffering from Spinal Disease and Fright	0	1	1
Uterine Disease and Irritation	0	2	2
,, ,, ,, General Bad Health	0	1	1
,, Irritation and Fright	0	1	1
Consequences of a Fall when a Child	0	1	1
Nervous Debility and Bad Health	0	2	2
Superannuation of Old Age and Morbis Cordis	0	1	1
Previous Illness	2	1	3
,, ,, Over-exertion and Debility	0	1	1
,, and Over-exertion	1	0	1
,, ,, ,, Childbirth	0	1	1
,, ,, ,, Hereditary	0	1	1
Hereditary	2	0	2
,, and Bad Health	0	1	1
,, ,, Poverty	0	1	1
Poverty and Imprisonment for Theft	0	1	1
,, ,, Loss of Sight	0	1	1
,, ,, Insufficient Food	1	0	1
Eating Adulterated Food	1	0	1
Intemperance	3	0	3
,, and Poverty	1	0	1
Excesses and Free Living	1	0	1
Irregular Mode of Life	0	1	1
,, ,, ,, ,, and Anxiety	1	0	1
,, ,, ,, ,, ,, Injury to Head	0	1	1
Congenital	5	1	6
Fright	0	1	1
,, at Sudden Death of Friends in Coal Mines	2	0	2
,, ,, Loosing her Friends in Manchester	0	1	1
Disappointment in Love	0	2	2
,, ,, Marriage and Seduction	0	2	2
Seduction and Bad Health	0	1	1
Religious Fanaticism	1	1	2
Remorse at Committing Murder and Epilepsy	1	0	1
Anxiety	0	1	1
,, about Loss of Sheep	1	0	1
,, ,, Means of Subsistence	1	1	2
,, ,, Loss of Money	0	2	2
,, ,, Misconduct of Child (poaching)	0	1	1
,, ,, Safety of Brother (Soldier)	0	1	1
Nursing Bed-ridden Father and Previous Illness	1	0	1
,, Husband and Inflammation of Chest	0	1	1
,, ,, ,, Previous Illness	0	1	1
Domestic Quarrels	0	2	2
,, ,, and Previous Illness	0	1	1
,, ,, ,, Misconduct of Wife	1	0	1
Loss of Money and Want of Employment	1	0	1
,, ,, ,, ,, Domestic Difficulties	1	0	1
,, ,, ,, ,, Anxiety	1	0	1
Desertion of Wife	1	0	1
,, ,, Husband and Syphilis	0	1	1
,, ,, ,, Childbirth	0	1	1
Unknown	7	6	13
Total	40	52	92
Hereditary Predisposition known to exist in the cases of	4	13	17

Left margin category labels: Physical, Moral.

TABLE VII.—*Illustrative of Suicidal Tendency in those admitted.*

	Males.	Females.	Total.
Have attempted Suicide	9	11	20
„ meditated „	9	14	23
Total	18	25	43
Form of Insanity during which Suicide was attempted—			
Mania, Acute	3	3	6
„ Chronic	1	3	4
„ Hysteric	0	1	1
„ with Epilepsy	2	0	2
„ „ General Paralysis ...	1	0	1
Melancholia	1	4	5
Monomania of Fear	1	0	1
Form of Insanity during which Suicide was meditated—			
Mania, Acute	1	4	5
„ Chronic	0	3	3
„ Recurrent	0	1	1
„ with Epilepsy	1	1	2
„ „ General Paralysis ...	1	0	1
Melancholia	2	1	3
Monomania of Suspicion	0	1	1
„ „ Superstition	1	0	1
„ „ Unseen Agency ...	0	2	2
„ „ Fear	1	0	1
Amentia	2	0	2
„ with Epilepsy	0	1	1
Means used in attempts made—			
Abstinence from Food	2	1	3
„ and Precipitation	1	0	1
„ „ Strangulation ...	0	1	1
Strangulation	1	1	2
„ and Cutting Throat ...	1	0	1
„ „ Precipitation ...	0	1	1
Precipitation	1	3	4
„ and Drowning	1	0	1
Drowning	1	4	5
Unknown	1	0	1

TABLE VIII.—*Occupations of those admitted.*

	Males.	Females.	Total.
Awl Blade Maker	1	0	1
Boatmen, Wives of	0	2	2
Butler	1	0	1
Button Maker	0	1	1
Carpenters	2	0	2
Carter, Wife of	0	1	1
Charwoman	0	1	1
Dressmakers	0	3	3
Druggist	1	0	1
Farmer	1	0	1
Foundryman	1	0	1
Gloveress	0	1	1
Grocer	1	0	1
Hedge Carpenter	1	0	1
Labourers, & Wives & Daughters of...	13	10	23
Land Surveyor	1	0	1
Laundress	0	1	1
Leather Grounder	1	0	1
Lodging-house Keeper	0	1	1
Miners, and Wife of	4	1	5
Nailers	1	2	3
Needle Straightener	0	1	1
„ Maker, Wife & Daughter of 10.	0	2	2
Plasterer	1	0	1
Printer, Wife of	0	1	1
Schoolmistresses	0	2	2
Seamstresses	0	3	3
Servants, Domestic	0	10	10
„ Gentleman's	1	0	1
Shoebinder	0	1	1
Shopkeeper and Wife of	1	1	2
Shepherd	1	0	1
Skinner	1	0	1
Spade Maker	1	0	1
Tradesmen, Wives of	0	2	2
Weaver	1	0	1
Washerwoman	0	1	1
Woolcomber	1	0	1
None	3	4	7
Total	40	52	92

TABLE IX.—*Showing the Condition of those admitted in reference to Education.*

	Males.	Females.	Total.
Fair Education	3	5	8
Can Read and Write	11	16	27
Can Read only...	16	19	35
Can neither Write nor Read	5	9	14
Unknown	5	3	8
Total	40	52	92

TABLE X.—*Showing the Social Condition of those admitted.*

	Males.	Females.	Total.
Married	16	22	38
Single	18	24	42
Widowers and Widows	4	6	10
Unknown	2	0	2
Total	40	52	92

TABLE XI.—*Showing the Religious Persuasion of those admitted.*

	Males.	Females.	Total.
Established Church	18	20	38
Protestant Dissenters	9	18	27
Methodists	3	9	12
„ Primitive	1	1	2
Independents	0	1	1
Baptists	1	0	1
Roman Catholics	0	2	2
Quakers	1	0	1
None or unascertained	7	1	8
Total	40	52	92

TABLE XII.—*Duration of Disease previous to admission in those discharged Cured.*

	Males.	Females.	Total.
Under 1 month	6	7	13
„ 2 months	3	2	5
„ 3 „	2	3	5
„ 6 „	0	1	1
„ 9 „	0	3	3
„ 12 „	0	1	1
For several years	0	1	1
Unknown	1	1	2
Total	12	19	31

TABLE XIII.—*Ages of those admitted and discharged Cured during the year.*

	ADMITTED.			DISCHARGED CURED.		
	Males.	Females.	Total.	Males.	Females.	Total.
From 5 to 10 years	1	0	1	0	0	0
„ 10 „ 20 „	1	7	8	0	4	4
„ 20 „ 30 „	7	11	18	3	5	8
„ 30 „ 40 „	7	15	22	0	5	5
„ 40 „ 50 „	6	11	17	3	3	6
„ 50 „ 60 „	11	2	13	5	1	6
„ 60 „ 70 „	3	5	8	1	1	2
„ 70 „ 80 „	4	1	5	0	0	0
Total	40	52	92	12	19	31

TABLE XIV.—*Period of Residence of those discharged Cured.*

	Males.	Females.	Total.
Under 2 months	3	1	4
„ 3 „	3	0	3
„ 6 „	1	5	6
„ 9 „	2	5	7
„ 12 „	0	4	4
„ 1 year and 3 months ...	1	2	3
„ 2 years	1	1	2
„ 3 „	1	0	1
„ 6 „	0	1	1
Total	12	19	31

TABLE XV.—*Form of Disease in those discharged Cured.*

	Males.	Females.	Total.
Mania, Acute	8	5	13
„ Hysteric	0	3	3
„ Chronic	1	0	1
„ Recurrent	0	1	1
„ with Paralysis...	1	1	2
Melancholia	2	5	7
Monomania	0	1	1
Dementia	0	2	2
„ with Hysteric Epilepsy ...	0	1	1
Total	12	19	31

TABLE XVI.—*Of 92 Patients admitted in 1858.*

	Males.	Females.	Total.
There have been Discharged Cured ...	5	7	12
„ „ „ Unimproved	1	0	1
„ Died	5	3	8
Remaining under treatment	29	42	71
Total	40	52	92

TABLE XVII.—*Showing the state of the Bodily Health and Condition of those admitted on their arrival at the Asylum.*

	Males.	Females.	Total.
1st. In good health and condition ...	11	11	22
2nd. In indifferent health and feeble } condition	23	35	58
3rd. In bad health and exhausted } condition	6	6	12
Total	40	52	92
2nd. Indifferent health and feeble condition, the results of—			
Mental State	4	2	6
„ „ and Febrile Disturbance } of System	2	2	4
„ „ „ Catarrh	1	0	1
„ „ Bronchitis and Asthma	1	2	3
„ „ and General Paralysis	4	0	4
„ „ „ Epilepsy	2	4	6
„ „ „ Chorea	0	1	1
„ „ „ Diarrhœa	1	1	2
„ „ „ Anæmia & Torpor } of Calculations	2	7	9
„ „ „ Morbus Cordis ...	0	1	1
„ „ „ Uterine Disease ...	0	3	3
„ „ Uterine Disease, and } Dyspepsia ...	0	2	2
„ „ and Dyspepsia	2	0	2
„ „ Hysteria and Debility	0	5	5
„ „ and Fever after Con- } finement ...	0	2	2
„ „ Defective Nutrition and } Exposion to Cold	4	3	7
Total	23	35	58
3rd. Bad health and exhausted condition, the results of—			
Mental State, General Functional } Disturbance, and Morbus Cordis	1	0	1
Mental State, General Functional } Disturbance, and Dyspepsia	1	0	1
Mental State and Abstaining from Food	1	0	1
Mental State and Abstaining from } Food, with Uterine Disease	0	2	2
Mental State and Disease of Spine } and Liver ...	0	1	1
„ „ Epilepsy, and Disease } of Spleen ...	1	0	1
„ „ and General Paralysis	1	2	3
„ „ Erysipelas, & Typhoid } Condition ...	0	1	1
„ „ Morbus Cordis, and } Paralysis ...	1	0	1
Total	6	6	12

TABLE XVIII.—*Causes of Death.*

	Males.	Females.	Total.
Exhaustion from General Paralysis ...	2	1	3
Exhaustion from General Paralysis and Mania	2	0	2
Exhaustion from General Paralysis, Diarrhœa, and Bed Sores ...	3	1	4
Cerebral Congestion and Pneumonia	1	0	1
Meningitis	0	1	1
Epilepsy and Rupture of Spleen during Fit	1	0	1
„ „ Disease of Heart ...	0	1	1
„ „ Asphyxia (dying during Fit)	0	1	1
Disease of Supra Renal Capsicles ...	0	1	1
Phlebitis	1	0	1
Gastro Enteritis	1	0	1
Phthisis	1	3	4
Exhaustion from Abstinence and Mania	0	1	1
Exhaustion from Abstinence and Melancholia	1	0	1
Exhaustion from Mania and Tabes Mesenterica	1	0	1
Exhaustion from Mania, Bronchitis, and Old Age	0	2	2
Exhaustion from Spinal and Liver Disease	0	1	1
Asphyxia by Drowning	1	0	1
Total	15	13	28

TABLE XIX.—*Ages of Patients Deceased.*

	Males.	Females.	Total.
From 10 to 20 years of age	0	1	1
„ 20 to 30 „ „	1	1	2
„ 30 to 40 „ „	6	2	8
„ 40 to 50 „ „	5	2	7
„ 50 to 60 „ „	3	2	5
„ 60 to 70 „ „	0	2	2
„ 70 to 80 „ „	0	2	2
„ 90 to 100 „ „	0	1	1
Total	15	13	28

TABLE XX.—*Period of Residence of those Deceased.*

	Males.	Females.	Total.
Under 1 day ...	1	0	1
„ 1 week ...	0	1	1
„ 2 weeks	0	1	1
„ 6 „ ...	1	0	1
„ 3 months	2	1	3
„ 4 „	2	0	2
„ 6 „	1	0	1
„ 10 „	1	0	1
„ 11 „	1	0	1
From 1 to 2 years	3	3	6
„ 2 to 3 „	1	2	3
„ 3 to 4 „	1	3	4
Under 6 years...	1	2	3
Total..	15	13	28

TABLE XXI.—*Duration of Disease previous to admission in those Deceased.*

	Males.	Females.	Total.
Under 1 month	5	4	9
„ 2 months	2	3	5
„ 3 „	1	0	1
„ 6 „	2	2	4
„ 1 year ...	1	0	1
„ 2 years...	0	1	1
„ 3 „ ...	0	1	1
For several years	2	0	2
Congenital	1	1	2
Unknown	1	1	2
Total ...	15	13	28

TABLE XXII.—*Form of Mental Disease in those Deceased.*

	Males.	Females.	Total.
Mania, Acute	1	2	3
„ Chronic	1	2	3
„ Hysteric	0	1	1
„ with Epilepsy	2	1	3
„ „ General Paralysis ...	5	1	6
Dementia	0	2	2
„ with General Paralysis ...	2	1	3
„ „ Epilepsy	0	1	1
„ Senile	0	1	1
Melancholia	2	0	2
Monomania	1	1	2
Idiocy	1	0	1
Total	15	13	28

TABLE XXIII.—*Form of Mental Disease of those remaining in the Asylum on the 31st December, 1858.*

	Males.	Females.	Total.
Mania, Acute ...	6	11	17
„ Chronic	11	27	38
„ Recurrent	10	19	29
„ Hysteric	0	5	5
„ Puerperal	0	1	1
„ with Paralysis	1	0	1
„ „ General Paralysis	8	5	13
„ „ Epilepsy	13	8	21
Dementia ...	10	22	32
„ Advanced ...	40	29	69
„ Senile ...	1	2	3
„ with Paralysis	3	1	4
„ „ General Paralysis	5	2	7
„ „ Epilepsy	9	7	16
Melancholia ...	8	8	16
Monomania of Pride ...	6	5	11
„ „ Suspicion	9	6	15
„ „ Superstition ...	3	1	4
„ „ Witchcraft ...	1	1	2
„ „ Unseen Agency	1	2	3
„ „ Fear ...	2	1	3
Amentia (Imbecility)...	4	3	7
„ „ with Epilepsy ...	3	0	3
„ (Idiotcy) ...	6	4	10
„ „ with Epilepsy ...	5	9	14
Total ...	165	179	344

TABLE XXIV.—*Showing the duration of the Mental Disease of those remaining in the Asylum on the 31st of December, 1858.*

	Males.	Females.	Total.
Under 3 months	2	3	5
„ 6 „	3	4	7
„ 9 „	5	8	13
„ 12 „	4	5	9
„ 18 „	3	8	11
„ 2 years...	9	8	17
„ 3 „	11	16	27
„ 4 „	7	9	16
„ 5 „	7	11	18
From 5 to 10 years	34	29	63
„ 10 to 15 „	27	30	57
„ 15 to 20 „	12	8	20
„ 20 to 25 „	8	5	13
„ 25 to 30 „	1	1	2
„ 30 to 35 „	1	3	4
„ 35 to 40 „	1	0	1
Under 50 years	0	1	1
For years (undefined)	9	11	20
Congenital	16	13	29
Unknown	5	6	11
Total	165	179	344

TABLE XXV.—*Showing the Ages of those remaining in the Asylum on the 31st of December, 1858.*

	Males.	Females.	Total.
From 5 to 10 years of age	1	0	1
„ 10 to 15 „	1	1	2
„ 15 to 20 „	4	7	11
„ 20 to 25 „	9	9	18
„ 25 to 30 „	18	14	32
„ 30 to 35 „	17	26	43
„ 35 to 40 „	22	19	41
„ 40 to 45 „	21	14	35
„ 45 to 50 „	19	27	46
„ 50 to 55 „	16	20	36
„ 55 to 60 „	7	22	29
„ 60 to 65 „	10	4	14
„ 65 to 70 „	10	11	21
„ 70 to 75 „	6	3	9
„ 75 to 80 „	4	1	5
„ 80 to 85 „	0	1	1
Total	165	179	344

TABLE XXVI.—*Showing the number of probably Curable and Incurable Patients remaining in the Asylum on the 31st of December, 1858.*

	Males.	Females.	Total.
Curable	18	33	51
Incurable	147	146	293
Total	165	179	344

Matron's Return of Female Patients Employed during the year ending December 31st, 1858.

How Employed.	No. of Days.
Sewing	17,367
Knitting	591
Washing and Ironing	9,949
Assisting Attendants	5,464
„ In the Kitchen	1,641
„ Housemaids	384
Total number of Days...	35,396
Weekly Average	681
Daily „	113
Employed 66 per cent. of the average number resident throughout the year.	

Head Attendant's Return of Male Patients Employed during the year ending December 31st, 1858.

How Employed.	No. of Days.
Tailors	2,855
Shoemakers	2,238
Carpenters	855
Smiths	1,444
Painters and Glaziers	1,436
Masons, Bricklayers, and Plasterers	500
Bakers and Brewers	944
Clerks	318
Hair-pickers	1,283
Assisting Attendants	5,853
„ on Farm or Garden	12,994
Total number of Days...	30,720
Weekly Average	590
Daily „	98
Employed 62 per cent. of the average number resident throughout the year.	

H

Unions Chargeable for the Patients remaining in the
Asylum on the 31st of December, 1858.

Males.	Females.	Chargeable to	Totals.
25	33	Worcester Union	58
17	21	Kidderminster ditto	38
30	0	Bedford County Asylum	30
6	18	Dudley Union	24
7	15	Stourbridge ditto	22
7	14	Upton-on-Severn ditto	21
9	12	Pershore ditto	21
10	10	King's Norton ditto	20
9	10	Bromsgrove ditto	19
9	7	Droitwich ditto	16
8	5	Westbromwich ditto	13
5	7	Martley ditto	12
4	8	Evesham ditto	12
3	3	Shipston-on-Stour ditto	6
1	5	Alcester ditto	6
3	2	County of Worcester	5
2	2	Tenbury Union	4
3	1	City of Worcester	4
3	0	Cleobury Mortimer Union	3
1	1	Tewkesbury ditto	2
1	0	Ledbury ditto	1
0	1	Hayfield ditto	1
0	1	Solihull ditto	1
1	0	Newent ditto	1
0	1	Dursley ditto	1
0	1	Clifton ditto	1
1	0	Glanford Brigg	1
0	1	Private Patient	1
165	179		344

Statement showing the Numbers of Lunatics and Idiots chargeable to the several Unions in the County and City of Worcester, and showing whether confined in Asylums or otherwise up to 1st January, 1859.

Unions.	In County and City Asylum.		In other Asylums.		In Work-houses.		With Friends.		Totals.		
	Males.	Females.	Males.	Females.	Males.	Females.	Males.	Females.	Males.	Females.	Totals.
1 Alcester	1	5	0	0	0	0	0	0	1	5	6
2 Bromsgrove ...	9	10	0	0	7	10	7	5	23	25	48
3 Bromyard	0	0	0	0	0	0	0	1	0	1	1
4 Cleobury Mortimer	3	0	0	0	0	0	0	0	3	0	3
5 Droitwich	9	7	0	1	2	4	5	7	16	19	35
6 Dudley	6	19	0	0	1	5	6	3	13	27	40
7 Evesham	4	8	0	0	1	3	2	2	7	13	20
8 Kidderminster..	17	21	0	0	14	8	3	3	34	32	66
9 King's Norton...	9	10	0	0	1	0	1	1	11	11	22
10 Ledbury	1	0	0	0	0	0	0	0	1	0	1
11 Martley	5	7	0	0	7	4	2	7	14	18	32
12 Newent	1	0	0	0	0	0	0	3	1	3	4
13 Pershore	9	12	0	0	0	0	1	2	10	14	24
14 Shipston-on-Stour	3	3	1	0	2	0	0	1	6	4	10
15 Solihull	0	1	0	0	1	0	0	0	1	1	2
16 Stourbridge	7	15	0	0	2	4	2	3	11	22	33
17 Stow-on-the-Wold.........	0	0	0	0	0	0	0	0	0	0	0
18 Stratford-on-Avon.........	0	0	0	0	1	0	0	0	1	0	1
19 Tenbury	2	2	0	0	0	1	2	2	4	5	9
20 Tewkesbury ...	1	1	0	0	0	0	0	1	1	2	3
21 Upton-on-Severn	8	14	0	0	2	4	9	9	19	27	46
22 Westbromwich ..	8	5	0	0	0	0	0	0	8	5	13
23 Worcester	25	33	0	0	1	4	1	2	27	39	66
City of Worcester	3	1	0	0	0	0	0	0	3	1	4
County of Worcester ..	2	2	0	0	0	0	0	0	2	2	4
Totals	133	176	1	1	42	47	41	52	217	276	493

Work Made and Repaired by the Female Patients, *from the*
1st January to the 31st December, 1858.

	Made.	Repaired.
Shirts	550	1,462
Flannel ditto	96	60
Pairs Trowsers	76	0
Ditto Drawers	120	64
Ditto Hose	60	6,420
Vests	138	0
Handkerchiefs	500	0
Neckerchiefs	416	0
Dresses	450	2,624
Night ditto	120	64
Petticoats	366	420
Chemises	400	2,416
Flannel ditto	40	94
Caps	244	694
Pinafores	124	84
Aprons	250	129
Pairs Stays	50	46
Bonnets (cotton)	69	0
Jerseys	30	24
Sheets	986	1,216
Pillow-cases	816	119
Rugs	0	169
Strong ditto	10	12
Table Cloths	50	18
Towels	452	12
Cushions	80	0
Curtains	44	0
Mattresses	180	79
Blankets	0	48
Blinds	24	0
Shrouds	20	0

Return of Work done by Tradesmen and Male Patients,
from 1st January to 31st December, 1858.

	Made.	Repaired.
Tailor's and Upholsterer's Shop.		
Coats	186	445
Vests	281	449
Trousers	286	636
Caps	295	0
Braces	152 Pairs	0
Hair Mattresses	95	66
Sea Grass ditto	96	18
Bolsters	36	4
Cushions for Seats	47	21
Ottomans	12	0
Waterproof Covers	20	38
Padded Frames, Stuffed	1 Set	0
Sofas, ditto	7	0
Carpets and Hearth-rugs	16	4
Window Blinds and Furniture	29	0
Canvas Stretchers	15	0
Shoemaker's Shop.		
Boots	124 Pairs	479 Pairs
Shoes	110 ,,	197 ,,
Slippers	123 ,,	94 ,,
Children's Shoes	21 ,,	21 ,,
Boot Laces	122 Doz. Pairs	Engine and Machine Belts ... 10
Belts for Attendants' Keys, &c.	48	Saddlery, Gearing, &c. &c.

Return of Work done by Tradesmen and Male Patients, &c., Continued.

	Made.	Repaired.
Engineer's Shop.	Making a complete Set of Ironwork for 24 New Wheelbarrows. Making one pair 3.2 Iron Pulley Block and Snatch Block. Casing with Sheet Iron 2 Dust Carts for Male and Female Divisions. Making 1 Iron Wheelbarrow for Gas-works Making 2 six-feet Iron Seats for Airing Courts. Replacing 150 feet of 1¼-inch Hot-water Pipes for No. 4 Male Ward. Making 5 New Wrought-iron Fire-guards, tipped with Brass, for Male and Female Wards. Making 120 Italian Irons for Laundry. New Laying with Steel and Dressing 110 Pickaxes for Navvy Work on the Estate. Making 12 Wrought-iron Music Stands for the Band. Making Drop Bolts and other Ironwork for large Gates at Farm Buildings. Making a complete Set of Ironwork, Fixing Mouth-pieces and Pipes to 2 Retorts at Gas-house. Making 8 Lead Waste Pipes and Fixing the same to Washing Troughs in Laundry. Making a complete Set of Ironwork for Water Gauges of Cooking Boilers. Making Ironwork for Door in Brewhouse. Making Ironwork for fixing Pads in Padded Room. Making a New Rack and Spindle for Scuffle for the Farm. Making 4 dozen Screw-pins for Locks. Taking out Old Hot-water Expansion Pipes and Refixing New on Male side of Asylum. Fixing a New Set of Gutta Percha Pipes to Beer-engine. Taking out the Boiling Furnace in Wash-house and Fixing New Pipes to the same. Making the Ironwork for Lightning Conductor at New Chapel. Making a New Copper Clack Valve, and Lengthening Handle of Pump at the Farm. Making Ironwork for small Gate at ditto. Fixing a New Wrought-iron Front to Grate in Steward's Office, also in Male Ward No. 3; taking down and Repairing Beer-engine.	Fitting up New Brasses, Connecting and Guide Rods to Steam Engine. Repairing Pumps at Gas-house and Farm Buildings. Repairing the Purifiers at the Gas-house Repairing the Bells on Female Division. Repairing Ironing Stove in Laundry, and Hot Plates in the Cooking Kitchen. Repairing small Force Pumps in connection with Engine. Repairing Cooking Range in Superintendent's House. Repairing Locks and Keys throughout the Asylum and different Offices thereto. Keeping in good repair the entire Gas Fittings of the Asylum. Repairing the Laundry and Engine-house Machinery. Tin-ware and Ironmongery for Kitchen and Steward's Stores. Garden and Farming Implements, including Ploughs, Harrows, Scuffles, Forks, Grapes, Spades, Carts, &c. &c. High and Low Pressure Boilers, Tubes, Gauges, and Safety-valves.

Return of Work done by Tradesmen and Male Patients, &c., Continued.

Made.	Repaired.
Engineer's Shop continued. Making and Fixing a two-burner Gas-light for the Cooking Kitchen. Making and Laying-on 3 Gas-lights to Carpenter's Shop. Taking out Old Slate Water Cistern over Bakehouse and Fitting Supply Pipes from Main. Fixing Gas-light in the Matron's Drawing-room. Making the entire Ironwork for New Oven in Bakehouse. Making Stoking Rods for Engine Boilers, Gashouse, and Laundry Stoves. Making Plugs for Steam Boilers. „ Mason's and Coal Hammers. „ Reels for Garden Lines. „ Baker's Peels, &c. &c.	Cisterns, Pipes, and Brasses to Lavatories, Pantries, Urinals, &c. &c. The entire Tools required by the different Workshops connected with the Asylum. Supply Boxes, Tanks, Taps, &c. &c. Iron Casements & Fittings thereto throughout the Asylum. Retorts, Coking Rods, Furnaces, &c. &c., for Gas-works and Laundry. Sundries, Cold and Hot Water Taps in connection with Bath-rooms, Washing Basins, &c.
Carpenter's Shop. 1 Mahogany Wardrobe, 1 Deal ditto, 2 Mahogany Night-commodes, for Superintendent's House. 1 Large Bookcase with Wings, Wirework, &c., complete, for Library. 2 Large Bookcases in Steward's Offices for the general Records of the Institution. 250 Picture Frames for Engravings to Wards, &c. &c. 2 Large Wardrobes for Female Wards, 400 feet Woodwork. 5 Cupboards in Ward Pantries, 5 ditto in Lavatories—total, 750 feet Woodwork. 1 French Bedstead made, 36 American Birch Bedsteads made, complete for Male and Female Wards. Taking down, making, and replacing large Drum of Washing Machine in Laundry. 12 Ottomans for Female Wards.	The necessary Repairs to Bedsteads throughout the Asylum for the year. The Farm and Garden Tools and Implements repaired during the year. Lavatories, Pantries, and Water-closets kept in good repair. Tables, Chairs, Seats, Presses, Flooring, Skirtings,&c.,in Male and Female divisions. Fitting on Locks, Easing Doors, &c., throughout the Asylum and Farm Buildings. Stretchers, Water Beds, Canvas Frames, &c. Casings to Baths, Water-closets, &c. &c., on Male and Female Divisions.

Return of Work done by Tradesmen and Male Patients, &c., Continued.

	Made.	Repaired.
Carpenter's Shop continued.	4 Chests of Drawers for Male and Female Wards. 6 Work Tables for Female Wards, 8 Dressing Tables for ditto. 1 Large Press for Laundry. 6 Small Oak Tables, 4 large Dining ditto, for Male and Female Wards. 18 Seats with Backs for ditto, 24 Stuff-bottomed Chairs, 36 Easy Chairs, for Invalids. 2 Shoemakers' Seats, 1 New Door for Laundry, 1 New Water-closet. 3 New Sash Windows and general Repairs (including Doors, Flooring, Staircase, and Skirtings) at Steward's Residence.	Fencing on Farm Repaired, Posts and Rails, Gates, &c. Attending to Engineer, Mason, and Painter, in connexion with the necessary repairs throughout the Asylum, &c. &c. Benches, Summer Seats, and Verandas kept in good repair for the year. Sundries, Broom-handles, Pickaxes, Forks, Spades, &c. &c., made and repaired.
Mason's and Bricklayer's Shop.	480 yards square of Colouring to Corridors leading to the Male and Female Wards. Rebuilding Fireplaces to Drying Stoves in Laundry. Fixing Hot-air Stove in New Chapel. 340 feet run 4-in. Drain Pipes from ditto. Taking down and Rebuilding Furnaces at Farm Buildings. Taking down and Rebuilding Piers at Entrance Lodge and Farm Buildings. 66 yards square of Colouring in Matron's Apartments. Taking out and Replacing 2 New Gas Retorts at Gas-works; also 24 days' Scraping Down and Repainting Gasometer. Making Well for Lightning Conductor at New Chapel. 252 yards square of Colouring to Male Hospital. Setting Grate in Steward's Office. Taking down and Enlarging Oven in Bake-house. Making and Fixing New Urinal in Male Airing Court.	Repairing Plastering throughout Asylum. Repairing and Pointing Walls previous to Painting. Altering and Diverting Drains at Magistrates' Stables, Farm Buildings, &c. Opening Drains from Water-closets and Urinals. Cleaning out & Repairing Extraction Flues. Repairing Flues&Chimneys after Sweeps. Repairing Brickwork at Engine and Cooking Boilers. Repairing Gutters, Traps, Urinals, Overflows, and Waste Water Pipes. Slating, examining Roofs, Chimneys, & Hot-air Flues.

Return of Work done by Tradesmen and Male Patients, &c., Continued.

Made.	Repaired.
Painter's and Glazier's Shop.	
Varnishing 6 Sofas for Male and Female Wards; Painting and Graining in Oak 4 Chests of Drawers for ditto.	Preparing and Painting 66 Bedsteads for Female Wards.
Painted and Grained in Mahogany 8 large Chests for ditto.	Preparing and Painting Skylights in Passages leading to Cooking Kitchen.
Preparing, Painting in Bird's-eye Maple and Varnishing, Drawing-room in Superintendent's House.	Preparing and Painting Bath-rooms and Lavatories in Wards No. 1 Males and 1 and 3 Females.
Cleaning Paper and Examining Windows in ditto.	Painting, 2 coats in stone colour, the Walls, Graining in Oak and Varnishing Doors and Skirtings in Magistrates' Entrance-hall.
Varnished 6 Bedsteads for Wards.	
Notting, Priming, and Painting inside and out Veranda in Male Airing Court.	
Polishing and Glazing 139 Picture Frames for Wards.	Notting, Priming, and Painting Wardrobes in Female Wards Nos. 1 and 2.
Notting, Priming, and Painting inside and out Veranda in Female Airing Court.	Preparing, Painting, and Graining Bathroom and Lavatories in Male No. 5.
Painting, 2 coats, 35 Barrows for Navvy Work.	Painting 2 Single Rooms, and 2 Sets of Pads on Male and Female Divisions.
Notting, Painting, and Graining in Oak New Bookcase in Library.	
French Polishing Mahogany Wardrobe for Superintendent's House.	Repairing Painted Walls, &c., in Males No. 4.
3 Fire-guards painted green, 2 coats each.	Painting, Graining, & Varnishing Front Door, Magistrates' Entrance.
Preparing and Painting, 4 coats salmon colour, the Walls of Male Hospital.	Painting with Anticorrosive Paint, 3 coats, 180 yds. square, the Gasometer.
Doors and Skirtings of ditto Grained and Varnished ; also the Windows, Jambs, Piping, Ventilators, Bath-room, &c. (Painting 208 yards and Graining 90 yards).	Painting Fencing round Garden, also 8 Seats in Airing Courts.
Notting, Priming, and Painting 2 Wardrobes in Male and Female Wards.	Repairing and Soldering Lead Work in Box Bedsteads, Females No. 3.
Notting and Graining in Oak 2 Bookcases in Steward's Office ; also Varnishing Oak Paper on Walls of ditto.	

Return of Work done by Tradesmen and Male Patients, &c., Continued.

Made.	Repaired.
Painter's and Glazier's Shop continued. Scraping off old Colour, Preparing and Painting, 5 coats, the Walls of Cooking Kitchen; also the Dome of ditto, 4 coats; Graining and Varnishing Doors, Shelves, Dresser, Surbase, Clock Case, and Japanning Cooking Apparatus (total, 309 yards square plain Painting, 49 yards Granite, and 45 yards Oak Graining.) 9 Seats and 1 Box Painted and Varnished for Wards. Painting and Graining in Mahogany large Dressing Table in Ward No. 7, Females; Buckets, Scuttles, and Sundry other Jobs Painted and Lettered.	Preparing and Painting in Granite the Walls of Bath-rooms and Lavatories in Males No. 3 and Females No. 3; also the Woodwork Painted stone colour. 1,017 squares of Glass Glazed throughout the Asylum for the year. Repairing Gutters, Ledges, and Spouting on Roof of Asylum, Workshops, Farm Buildings, &c. Repairing Paperhangings, Colouring, and sundry Jobs during the year.

Salaries and Wages.

		Per Year.
		£
†Medical Superintendent		400
*Chaplain		50
*Clerk to Committee of Visitors		80
†Clerk and Steward of Asylum		110
Matron		60
†Engineer and Gatekeeper		60
Head Male Attendant		37
Attendant Male Carpenter		30
Ditto „ Mason and Bricklayer		30
Ditto „ Tailor		30
Ditto „ Painter and Glazier...		27
Ditto „ Shoemaker		26
One Male Attendant		29
One „ „		27
Three „ „		26
One „ „		25
One Female Attendant		15
One „ „		14
Four „ „		13
Four „ „		12
Night Nurse		16
Cook		16
Kitchenmaid		10
Housemaid		11
Laundress		20
First Laundrymaid		13
Second „		£11. 11s
Gardener		30
Baker and Brewer		27
Stoker		23
Farm Servant		19
Ditto Labourer		13
Groom		10

(Staff)

	Per Week.
*Carpenter	20s.
Jobbing Carpenter	10s.
*Cowman	12s.
*Labourer	12s.
Upholsterer	11s.

(Workmen.)

Without a mark, have Bed, Board, and Washing.
*Non-resident.
†Have Furnished House, Gas, Fire, Vegetables, and Washing.

COUNTY AND CITY OF WORCEST

Income and Expenditure for

Heads of Income.	INCOME FOR THE QUARTER ENDING				
	March 31st.	June 30th.	September 30th.	December 31st.	Total for Year.
	£. s. D.	£. s. D.	£. s. D.	£. s. D.	£. s.
Worcester Union	303 9 10	299 12 6	309 11 3	319 4 11	1,231 18
Kidderminster	185 9 9	178 19 9	199 5 0	207 15 11	771 10
Dudley	138 0 11	133 15 0	144 15 0	140 7 8	556 18
Upton-on-Severn	101 15 7	117 6 3	128 6 3	106 12 7	454 0
Droitwich	121 8 5	85 1 6	98 16 0	97 17 11	403 3
Stourbridge	125 8 6	121 3 9	125 0 3	113 15 7	485 8
Pershore	139 19 6	126 2 6	126 15 0	125 3 11	518 0
Martley	77 18 3	73 18 9	73 9 9	40 16 3	266 3
Bromsgrove	93 15 11	88 18 9	108 7 3	100 17 7	391 19
Evesham	67 3 10	64 0 0	70 2 6	66 15 11	268 2
West Bromwich	81 4 10	83 8 6	83 6 0	74 11 7	322 10
Ledbury	6 2 2	5 13 9	5 15 0	5 11 9	23 2
Tenbury	12 4 4	18 6 2	17 5 0	20 15 5	68 10
Shipston-on-Stour	30 10 10	32 11 3	34 10 0	33 10 6	131 2
Alcester	32 15 7	31 7 6	34 10 0	33 10 6	132 3
King's Norton	91 12 6	89 6 0	89 10 0	131 18 3	402 6
Cleobury Mortimer	12 4 4	12 2 6	17 5 0	16 15 3	58 7
Tewkesbury	6 2 2	5 13 9	5 15 0	16 18 6	34 9
Solihull	6 2 2	5 13 9	5 15 0	5 11 9	23 2
Newent	6 2 2	5 13 9	5 15 0	5 11 9	23 2
County of Worcester	29 10 5	19 8 6	17 19 9	19 14 10	86 13
City of Worcester	12 4 4	11 7 6	22 1 3	22 7 0	68 0
Out Counties:—					
Winchcomb Union, Gloucestershire	8 4 0	1 1 5	,, ,, ,,	. ,, ,, ,,	9 5
Dursley Union, ditto	11 3 2	8 2 6	8 4 3	8 4 3	35 14
Hayfield Union, Derbyshire	8 0 9	8 2 6	8 4 3	8 4 3	32 11
Eton Union, Bucks	3 9 7	,, ,, ,,	,, ,, ,,	,, ,, ,,	3 9
Whitchurch Union, Salop	8 0 9	2 1 11	,, ,, ,,	,, ,, ,,	10 2
Ludlow Union, Herefordshire	8 0 9	1 3 3	0 13 0	,, ,, ,,	9 17
St. Chad's Parish, Shrewsbury	4 7 5	,, ,, ,,	,, ,, ,,	,, ,, ,,	4 7
Glanford Brigg Union, Lincolnshire	8 0 9	8 2 6	8 4 3	8 4 3	32 11
County of Bedford	221 15 0	224 5 0	227 3 9	226 15 0	899 18
Melksham Union, Wiltshire	8 0 9	4 11 1	,, ,, ,,	,, ,, ,,	12 11
Clifton Union, Somersetshire	8 0 9	8 2 6	8 4 3	8 4 3	32 11
Taunton Union, ditto	,, ,, ,,	24 7 6	8 4 3	3 7 0	35 18
Bromyard Union, Herefordshire	,, ,, ,,	,, ,, ,,	,, ,, ,,	4 11 1	4 11
Private Patients	17 2 1	17 1 3	11 16 3	14 4 3	60 3
Sales from Farm and Stores	83 14 5	64 3 5	67 13 5	150 19 3	366 10
Refunded by County and City of Worcester — Repairs' Account	,, ,, ,,	53 12 6	19 10 0	20 15 10	93 18
Totals £	2,079 6 6	2,034 9 0	2,091 12 11	2,159 14 9	8,365 3

UPER LUNATIC ASYLUM.

r ending 31st December, 1858.

Heads of Expenditure.	EXPENDITURE FOR THE QUARTER ENDING														
	March 31st.			June 30th.			September 30th.			December 31st.			Total for the Year.		
	£.	s.	D.	£.	s.	D.	£.	s.	D.	£.	s.	D.	£.	s.	D.
ovisions—															
Meat and Bacon	238	18	5	287	1	2	299	8	0	309	8	0	1,184	15	7
Flour	171	17	6	172	13	0	178	0	0	148	16	0	671	6	6
Bread	"	"	"	"	"	"	"	"	"	11	3	4	11	3	4
Oatmeal, Barley, & Peas	16	6	1	3	10	9	18	9	1	"	"	"	38	5	11
Malt and Hops	152	2	9	80	0	0	78	6	8	186	12	0	497	1	5
Butter	32	11	11	33	19	5	37	16	10	54	6	2	158	14	4
Cheese	22	8	3	10	13	6	21	1	5	18	5	4	72	8	6
Tea and Coffee	46	4	1	65	18	11	44	9	8	24	16	2	181	8	10
Sugars	30	19	7	41	10	10	46	19	7	43	2	5	162	12	5
Mustard and Pepper	2	6	6	0	14	7	3	13	6	3	16	8	10	11	3
Wines and Spirits	24	3	0	32	10	6	33	6	0	29	2	2	119	1	8
Porter	1	14	0	0	18	0	32	6	6	14	4	6	49	3	0
Cider	"	"	"	"	"	"	17	6	3	8	12	11	25	19	2
Rice, Arrowroot, & Sago	22	1	6	8	16	4	8	10	0	1	3	4	40	11	2
Raisins and Currants	9	0	6	15	7	0	6	9	11	9	2	8	40	0	1
Potatoes and Fish	53	17	2	44	10	8	"	"	"	22	0	0	120	7	10
Eggs	1	15	9	2	5	0	3	13	9	3	6	6	11	1	0
Groceries (Sundries)	5	16	0	6	4	1	2	9	1	6	19	5	21	8	7
ouse Necessaries—															
Coals and Slack	101	7	5	73	5	0	173	14	1	153	9	11	501	16	5
Soaps and Soda	34	0	3	37	0	0	31	9	9	30	17	0	133	7	0
Starch and Blue	1	17	8	0	14	10	2	3	3	1	2	4	5	18	1
Candles	5	0	4	1	18	0	3	18	6	3	14	0	14	10	10
Brushes and Combs	5	16	7	7	4	1	8	7	0	10	14	6	32	2	2
House Flannel	4	19	0	6	0	0	4	0	0	"	"	"	14	19	0
atients' Clothing	175	17	0	191	13	7	217	0	3	176	19	11	761	10	9
edding and Linen	47	18	6	56	13	6	59	7	7	81	7	5	245	7	0
iscellaneous—															
Ironmongery	7	16	7	18	12	7	40	11	10	18	8	2	85	9	2
Earthenware and Glass	7	13	3	37	19	0	2	3	9	15	6	6	63	2	6
Rates and Taxes	5	1	2	7	13	7	4	11	2	6	13	0	23	18	11
Sundries	58	6	1	77	2	8	39	12	11	55	5	4	230	7	0
arm and Garden	70	12	11	100	17	5	149	18	3	101	5	6	422	14	1
alaries and Wages	355	10	10	358	19	5	355	2	0	360	6	0	1,429	18	3
Workmen's & Labourers' Wages	35	0	0	41	11	0	42	5	0	31	4	10	150	0	10
tationery, Postages, Printing, &c.	24	15	3	60	11	3	15	0	3	26	2	3	126	9	0
unerals, Removals, and Allowances, repaid in Maintenance Account	5	17	0	5	14	0	3	16	0	9	3	5	24	10	5
Medicines and Surgical Instruments	26	13	9	24	12	4	28	15	1	44	9	6	124	10	8
Balances	272	19	11	119	16	0	77	10	0	138	7	7	608	10	6
Totals .... £	2,079	6	6	2,034	9	0	2,091	12	11	2,159	14	9	8,365	3	2

BALANC

General Statement of the Receipts and Payments on Account of

DR. 1st January

Receipts.	£.	s.
1st Jan., 1858:		
Balance in Treasurer's hands ... ... £1,815 8 8 ⎫	1,822	8
Ditto in Steward's hands ... ... 6 19 6 ⎭		
Receipts under the following heads, viz. :		
From Sales and Produce of Labour, &c.	366	10
Maintenance Account, viz.:		
From Private Patients	50	3
„ Unions and Parishes within the County	5,643	4
„ County of Worcester for Vagrants...	71	19
„ City of Worcester for ditto...	49	17
„ Out Counties and Boroughs (not contributing)	1,068	12
„ County and City Treasurers' for Repairs to Buildings, ⎫ Furniture, &c. &c. ... ... ⎭	885	2
Total	£9,957	18

Statement of the Financial Affairs of t

	£.	s.
1st Jan., 1859:		
Amount in Treasurer's hands ... ... £1,443 14 6 ⎫	1,448	19
Ditto in Steward's ditto ... ... 5 4 6 ⎭		
Ditto due from Unions and Parishes this day for Maintenance, &c., ⎫ of Patients ... ... ⎭	2,030	8
Total	£3,479	7

HEET.

unty and City of Worcester Pauper Lunatic Asylum, from st December, 1858.

CR.

𝔓aɒments.	£.	S.	D.
1st Jan., 1858:			
alance due to Treasurer	0	0	0
Payments under the following heads, viz.:			
alaries and Wages	1,429	18	3
rovisions	3,226	18	1
ines, Spirits, and Porter	160	4	6
ecessaries (Fuel, Light, and Washing)	747	13	5
urgery and Dispensary	113	3	4
lothing	747	8	9
urniture and Bedding	216	7	7
uneral Expenses (Repaid in Maintenance Account)	24	10	5
epairs to Building, Furniture, &c. &c.	885	2	10
arden and Farm	427	12	4
ates, Taxes, and Rent of Land	63	19	10
iscellaneous, Printing, Stationery, Freights, Postages, Books for Library, &c. &c.	466	0	7
31st Dec., 1858:	8,508	19	11
alance in Treasurer's hands £1,443 14 6	1,448	19	0
itto in Steward's ditto 5 4 6			
Total	£9,957	18	11

Institution on the 1st January, 1859.

	£.	S.	D.
1st Jan., 1859:			
mount due to Tradesmen this day on account of Patients' Maintenance, &c.	1,526	15	5
urplus available	1,952	12	1
Total	£3,479	7	6

1858.

DIETARY.

Days of the Week.	BREAKFAST.		DINNER.		SUPPER.	
	Males.	Females.	Males.	Females.	Males.	Females.
SUNDAY	1 pint coffee, 8 oz. bread, ½ oz. butter.	1 pint coffee or tea, 6 oz. bread, ½ oz. butter.	6 oz. roast meat (cooked) without bone, 6 oz. bread, vegetables, ½ pint beer.	5 oz. roast meat (cooked) without bone, 4 oz. bread, vegetables, ½ pint beer.	1 pint tea, 8 oz. bread, ½ oz. butter.	1 pint tea, 8 oz. bread, ½ oz. butter.
MONDAY	1½ pint milk porridge, 8 oz. bread.	1 pint milk porridge, 6 oz. bread.	½ lb. rice or sago pudding, 8 oz. bread, ½ pint beer.	½ lb. rice or sago pudding, 6 oz. bread, ½ pint beer.	1 pint coffee, 8 oz. bread, ½ oz. butter.	„
TUESDAY	„	„	6 oz. boiled meat (cooked) without bone, 6 oz. bread, vegetables, ½ pint beer.	5 oz. boiled meat (cooked) without bone, 4 oz. bread, vegetables, ½ pint beer.	„	„
WEDNESDAY	„	„	1½ pint barley broth, 8 oz. bread, vegetables, ½ pint beer.	1 pint barley broth, 6 oz. bread, vegetables, ½ pint beer.	„	„
THURSDAY	„	„	Beef steak pie and Irish stew, each week alternate; 8 oz. bread, vegetables, ½ pint beer.	Beef steak pie and Irish stew, each week alternate; 6 oz. bread, vegetables, ½ pint beer.	„	„
FRIDAY	„	„	6 oz. boiled meat (cooked) without bone, 6 oz. bread, vegetables, ½ pint beer.	5 oz. boiled meat (cooked) without bone, 4 oz. bread, vegetables, ½ pint beer.	„	„
SATURDAY	„	„	1½ pint pea-soup, 8 oz. bread, vegetables, ½ pint beer.	1 pint pea-soup, 8 oz. bread, vegetables, ½ pint beer.	„	„

FEEBLE & SICK PATIENTS } Whatever is ordered by the Medical Superintendent.... } Chops, Steaks, Eggs, Fowl, Beef Tea, Essence of Beef, Sago, Arrow-root, Rice and Milk, Custard & Bread Pudding, Jellies, Wine, Spirits, & Porter, Extra Tea & Sugar, &c.

LUNCHEON ..... 4 oz. Bread, ¼ oz. Cheese, ½ pint Beer, at 11 o'clock a.m. } For Patients working in Wards, Kitchen, Laundry, Workshops, and on the Farm and Garden.

EXTRA .... ½ pint Cider or Beer .... 4 o'clock p.m.

verage Weekly Cost for Maintenance, Medicine, Clothing, and Care of Patients during the year 1858.

	s.	D.	
Provisions	3	9	22729
Clothing	0	10	56035
Salaries and Wages	1	8	2933
Necessaries (Fuel, Light, and Washing)	0	10	56427
Surgery and Dispensary	0	1	70154
Wine, Spirits, and Porter	0	2	29246
Furniture and Bedding	0	3	3619
Garden and Farm	0	6	106106
Miscellaneous	0	6	104328
	8	10	91679
Less Receipts from Sales, Produce of Labour, &c. ...	0	5	15932
Net Average Weekly Cost per head	8	5	$\frac{75747}{119966}$

Daily Average Number of Patients Resident...................... 328 $\frac{246}{365}$

Weekly charge for Patients belonging) First quarter of year, 9s. 6d.
to Unions and Parishes within the} Second and third ditto, 8s. 9d.
County ....) Fourth ditto, 8s. 6d.

Ditto from other Counties & Boroughs} 11s. 6d. and 12s. 6d.
(not contributing) ....}

Ditto for Private Patients ......average   8s. 10½d.

Contract Price of Articles for Consumption, &c.
1858.

Description.	Lady-day Quarter.	Midsummer Quarter.	Michaelmas Quarter.	Christmas Quarter.
Flour (Seconds), per sack, 280lbs.	40s.	35s.	33s.	33s.
,, (Thirds), ,,	37s.	32s.	30s.	30s.
Beef and Mutton (best), per lb. ...	5¼d.	5¼d.	5¼d. & 5⅝d.	5¼d. & 5½d.
Butter (Salt), per lb. ...	10½d. & 11d.	10½d.	10d. to 1s. & 8d. to 11d.	11½d.
Cheese, per lb. ...	4½d.	4d.	28s. to 48s. per cwt.	4d.
Tea, per lb. ...	2s. 11d.	2s. 10d.	2s. 11d.	2s. 10d.
Coffee, per cwt. ...	108s.	105s.	95s. to 108s.	90s.
Sugar (moist). per lb. ...	4½d.	43s. per cwt.	42s. per cwt.	4½d.
,, (lump). per lb. ...	6d.	6¼d.	6¼d.	6d.
Rice, per cwt. ...	13s. 6d.	13s. 6d.	12s.	11s. 6d.
Oatmeal, per cwt.	13s.	...	...	16s.
Split Peas, per cwt.	15s.	15s. 6d.	16s.	15s. 6d.
Barley (Pearl), per cwt. ...	19s.	16s.	16s.	15s. 6d.
Malt, per bushel ...	8s. 3d.	8s.	7s. 10d.	8s. 6d.
Coals (Household), per ton	14s. 6s.	15s.	14s. 6d.	14s. 6d.
Slack (Engine), per ton	10s.	9s. 6d.	9s. 6d.	9s. 6d.
Gas Coal (Durham), per ton	25s.	25s.	25s.	25s.
Soap (White), per cwt. ...	47s. 6d.	48s.	...	...
,, (Yellow), per cwt. ...	38s. 6d.	38s.	36s. 6d.	36s. 6d.
,, (Soft), per 60lbs. ...	16s.	17s.	14s.	14s.
Soda, per cwt. ...	7s. 4d.	7s. 3d.	6s. 3d.	8s. 6d.
Candles (Dips), per 12lbs.	6s. 4d.	6s. 4d.	6s. 3d.	6s. 2d.
Composites, per 12lbs. ...	9s. 2d.	...	8s. 10d.	8s. 10d.

General Statement of the Income and Expenditure on Account of the Farm and Garden for the year ending 31st December, 1858.

BALANCE SHEET.

Dr. Income.	£.	s.	D.	Cr. Expenditure.	£.	s.	D.
To Supplied Asylum:—				By Stock on hand beginning of the year	637	3	0
3,287 Gallons New Milk ...	125	0	0				
2,922 " Skimmed ditto	66	6	1				
882 lbs. Fresh Butter ...	55	4	4				
6 Dozen Eggs ...	0	5	9				
28 Fowls	2	16	0				
800 Gallons Cider & Perry	20	0	0				
Roots, Vegetables, Herbs, &c. &c.	220	0	0	" Lady-day Quarter—Seeds, Stock, Wages, Taxes, Rent of Land, Provender, &c.	99	17	2
1,327 lbs. Beef	30	8	2				
406 lbs. Veal	9	8	9				
To Sold:—							
171 Gallons New Milk ...	6	1	11				
260½ lbs. Fresh Butter ...	14	18	5	" Midsummer Quarter ...	130	7	0
3 Dozen Eggs ...	0	2	6				
38 Fowls	2	15	0				
4 Cows	39	7	0				
3 Calves	5	5	0	" Michaelmas Quarter ...	177	10	11
50 Pigs	95	11	4				
91½ Bushels Wheat ...	68	8	0				
1¼ Acre Peas ...	20	0	0	" Christmas Quarter ...	124	10	0
Hides and Fat	4	1	0				
Plants and Roots ...	1	0	0				
Sundries	0	17	6				
Value of Dead & Live Stock on hand end of the year }	689	12	0	" Balance (in favour) ...	308	0	8
	£1,477	8	9		£1,477	8	9

WORCESTER:
PRINTED BY CHALK AND HOLL, HERALD-OFFICE.